Dundee Street Songs, Rhymes and Games

*for Chris, with lots of love
with warmest wishes,
Margaret Bennett*

Dundee Street Songs, Rhymes and Games:
The William Montgomerie Collection, 1952

Introduced, transcribed and annotated by Margaret Bennett
Illustrated by Les McConnell

First published on 2021 by Grace Note Publications
Grange of Locherlour, Ochtertyre, PH7 4JS, Scotland

© Margaret Bennett and Les McConnell, 2021

The rights of the recording are retained
by the Estate of Norah and William Montgomerie

ISBN 978-1-913162-14-6

A catalogue record of this book is available from the British Library

Royal Conservatoire
of Scotland

Dundee Street Songs, Rhymes and Games

The William Montgomerie Collection, 1952

Margaret Bennett
Illustrated by Les McConnell

CONTENTS

CAPTURING THE SOUND OF THE VOICE

The Pioneering Folklorist	1
Norah and William Montgomerie	4
Folklorists and Scots language activists	6
Bill and Norah: Biographical sketches	8
From childhood in London to a career in Dundee	10
Meeting Bill	12
Collaborating and Collecting	13
Audio-recording the voices of tradition	14
Visiting a playground in Dundee	16
Using the Scots Language in the playground and in print	17
Notes	22

STREET SONGS, RHYMES AND GAMES

Introduction and Notes	33

SINGING GAMES & ACTION SONGS

1. Queen Mary, Queen Mary, my age is sixteen	39
2. All the boys in our town	40
3. Brown bread and brandy-o	40
4. Will ye lay the cushion doon?	41

5. The Hokey-Pokey   42
6. Meh Lad's a Terrie   43
7. The Banks o Aberfeldy   43
8. There Came Three Dukes a-riding   45

SKIPPING RHYMES & SONGS

9. A Sailor went to sea   49
10. Through the fields   49
11. As I climbed up a Chinese steeple   50
12. Bell-bottom trousers   50
13. Brush your boots and follow   51
14. Down in German-ay   51
15. Down in the meadow where the green grass grows   52
16. German boys they act so funny   52
17. Hill Street girls are happy   52
18. Hoppy-Hoppy is my Name   53
19. I Love Bananas   53
20. I'm a Girl Guide   53
21. I'm a little Dutch girl   54
22. Whaur hae you been aa the day?   54
23. Jelly on the plate   54
24. Little tin soldier stand at attention   55
25. Maypole butter, maypole tea   56
26. She can't go to school without   56
27 The Quartermaster's Store   57

STOTTIN THE BA: BALL BOUNCING GAMES

28. Stot, stot, ba, ba	61
29. Tensy, ninesy	61
30. I'm the Monster of Blackness	61
31. Over the garden wall	62
32. Archibald-bald, bald	62
33. The London ball	63
34. Are you going to golf, sir?	64
35. Charlie Chaplin went to France	65
36. Mademoiselle from Armetières	66
37. Alla Balla and the forty thieves	66
38 Robin Hood and his Merry Men	66

HAND-CLAPPING

39. The bumbee stung me	69
40. Up and down the ladder in the caravan	70
41. RAF o'er Berlin	70
42. Mary Queen of Scots got her head chopped off	71
43 Knaves and shepherds come away	71

PLAYGROUND SONGS and SINGING FOR FUN

44. I'm a sailor home from sea	75
45. Three wee wifes	77
46. I married a wife	78
47. Poor Lady Lido	80

NOTES ON THE SONGS, RHYMES AND GAMES 83

FURTHER READING & LISTENING

Books and cassettes for children, parents and teachers 109

Poetry by William Montgomerie 111

Research contributions by William Montgomerie 112

Citations and sources 114

Online resources 118

Song First Lines 119

Contributors 123

Acknowledgements 124

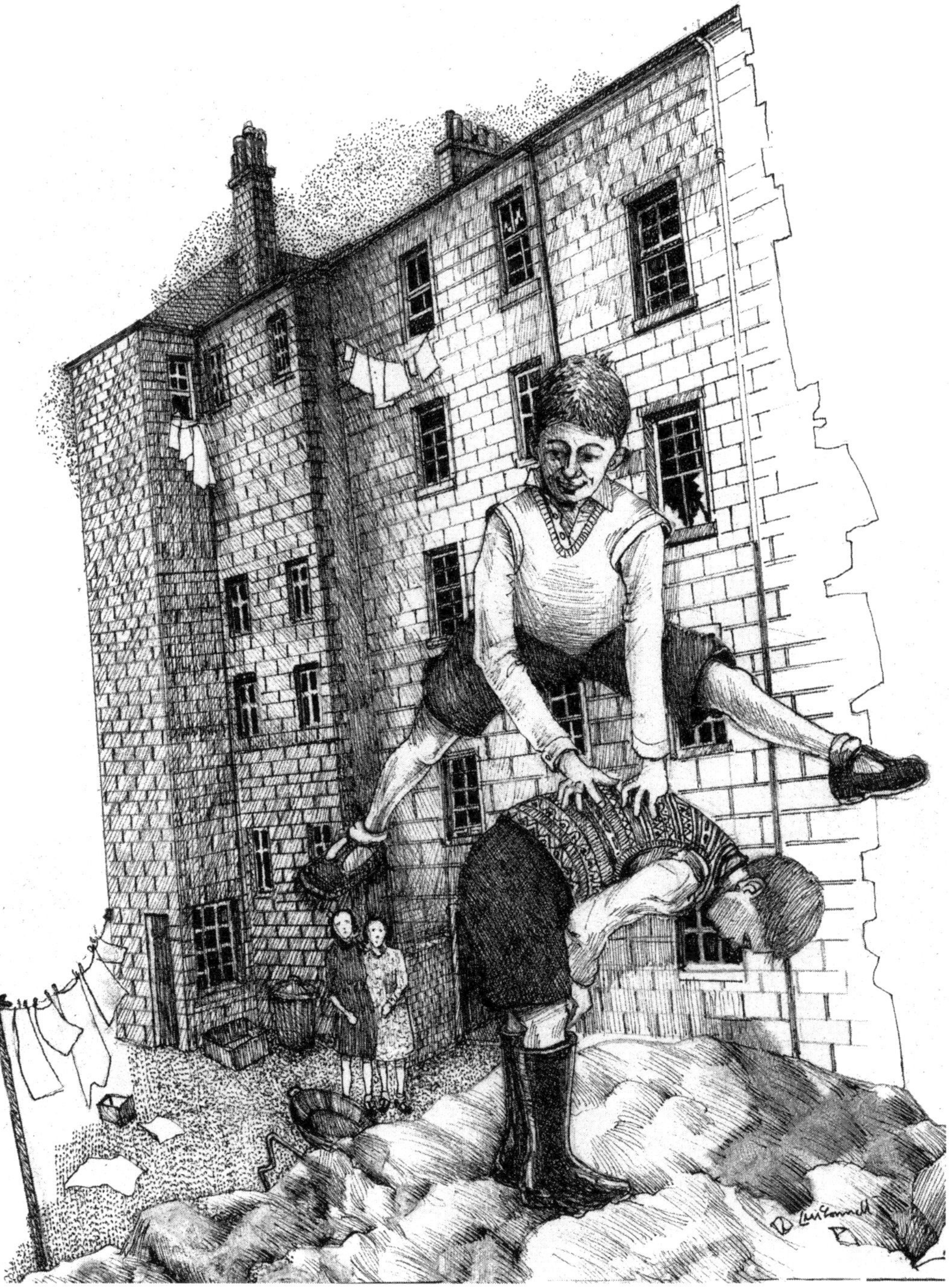

CAPTURING THE SOUND OF THE VOICE

The Pioneering Folklorists

> [T]he very greatest boon of the gramophone and phonograph is that they record not merely the tunes and words of fine folk-songs, but give an enduring picture of the lives, art and traditions ... of singing and fiddling ... dialects of different districts ... vocal habits and other personal characteristics of singers ... From his phonograph the collector can note down at full leisure, and with all possible care and thoroughness, repeating his records again and again, in part and in whole, until he has extracted from them a host of details that seem to him fascinating, interesting, or instructive.[1]
>
> Percy Grainger (1882–1961)

While the legendary Percy Grainger may be best remembered as a composer and arranger, he was also a dedicated folklorist who left a lasting legacy to folksong collecting and scholarship. He was a member of The Folk-Song Society (founded 1898) when, in 1906, he made his first fieldwork disc-recording using a 'Standard' Edison-Bell Phonograph machine, he hoped to convince fellow members — most of them highly competent musicians — of 'the incomparably greater scope' of machine over paper and pencil. He was 'surprised how very readily the old singers took to singing into
the machine' and excited that the fieldworker no longer has to 'interrupt the singer during his performance.' Grainger was in no doubt that song collectors would attain greater accuracy in transcription of words and music, particularly modal and gap-note melodies, rhythmic and dynamic contrasts, dramatic effects and all the 'meaningless syllables'.[2] But then as now, not everyone takes kindly to advice from a young, eccentric, upstart, and Cecil

Sharp (1859–1924), who had been collecting folksongs since 1903, wrote to Grainger: 'I am unable to endorse all that you say in its praise.'[3] Within a year, however, Sharp had followed Grainger's lead, and by 1908 Ralph Vaughan Williams had also adopted the new approach.

As far as the chronology of audio-recording goes, however, first off the mark was the secretary of the Folk-Song Society, Scottish-born Lucy Broadwood, who headed to the West Highlands of Scotland to record Gaelic songs in the Arisaig area. She used a wax cylinder recorder, and, shortly afterwards, Marjorie Kennedy Fraser made the first of several recording trips to the Outer Isles and Skye, where she began a monumental project to record Gaelic songs.[4] It was not until 1929 that wax cylinder was used to record Scots songs, when the visiting American James Madison Carpenter began a research project that would continue until he returned home in 1935.[5] Meanwhile, efforts to record Gaelic songs continued from the late 1920s with the work of John Lorne Campbell and his American wife, Margaret Fay Shaw.[6] They relied on 'pencil and paper' until 1937, when Campbell acquired his first audio-recording device: a clockwork Ediphone wax-cylinder recorder. Later that year, on a visit to America, he bought a disc-recording machine on which he made his now legendary recordings in Barra.[7] While there were huge advantages to these machines, yet both had their disadvantages: wax cylinders were fragile, and disc recorders were extremely heavy and difficult to use.

The invention of the wire-recorder opened up new prospects as it was portable, relatively easy to use, and capable of very good sound production. Developed in the 1930s in the lead-up to the Second World War, it was initially used for security purposes (spying and phone-tapping), and was not commercially available until the 1940s. A wire-recorder was not, however, the sort of purchase that most families would have considered, as many homes in Scotland did not have a radio (or wireless, as it was then called) until they saved up to buy one to hear the wartime news. In the mid-1940s, however, Dundee school-teacher William Montgomerie (1904–1998) bought a Wirex recorder as he saw it as the only way that he could *accurately* preserve the Scots language exactly as it was spoken or sung.

His daughter Dian (b. 1935) remembers the machine acquired during years of wartime rationing, when colour-coded coupon books governed the meagre amounts allowed for grocery-shopping, and 'mend and make do' became the norm for clothing; luxuries were out of the question, seldom a second helping at dinner-time, and no treats except the occasional 'quarter of sweeties' or small bar of chocolate the children shared on Saturday. Rationing lasted until 1954, yet Dian recalls that her parents seemed to regard this machine as essential, though it had no connection to her father's role as a school-teacher or to her mother's career as an artist.

Nevertheless, she and her brother Iain (b. 1940) understood why the new machine was so important to their parents — Bill and Norah always seemed to be working on a book, writing down every Scots rhyme, song, and saying they heard. Looking back on her childhood, Dian recalled that this 'fieldwork' even featured in their family weekends and holidays, when her father was especially single-minded:

> In the 1930s and 40s he pedalled around Angus, Perth, and Fife on his bicycle, [collecting and then] recording songs and lore on an old-fashioned wire machine, not graduating to the use of a car and a reel-to-reel tape recorder until the 1950s, when [in 1951 and 1955], along with Hamish Henderson, he worked with American folklorist Alan Lomax.[8]

The children's voices featured here were recorded in 1952 on a reel-to-reel tape recorder, which used acetate tape. It had a removable uptake reel (as opposed to a fixed reel), a better sound quality, tapes were easier to duplicate and edit than wire, and had none of the risk of tangling up wire finer than a fishing line. The setting was a playground in Hilltown, Dundee, one of the most densely populated areas of the city, and the date was Tuesday, June 24th, which was during the school term.

Most of the children attending the local school lived in nearby tenements, and, as 'Hilltown lassie' Lesley McLuckie recalls, the children all played and sang at the back of the tenements, as well as in the school playground. Listening to the William Montgomerie recordings for the first time (2020) she said the voices of the children brought back a flood of memories: "I was back in the fifties, in the Hilltoon, wi aa the bairns playin in the courties, up an doon the pletties, jumpin across air raid shelters in Kinghorne Road ... up the Laa wi pals, racin roon the Monument like aa the bairns afore us. An my Saturday treat wi Mum! She'd buy a cup o wulks an a peen fae the wifie selling them fae a barrow ..." Like many others of her generation, Lesley can still sing the songs and rhymes of childhood — "We were never done singing them ..."[9]

Now retired after a career in primary school teaching, Lesley imagines the children would have been amazed at anyone wanting to record them playing — they would also have been fascinated by the big tape-recorder. She herself was too young to have been among them, as "they sound like upper primary ... my cousin was in that age group .... There must be a few of them still around.... They'd all be up about eighty by now.... But who was the man who recorded them?"

William Montgomerie was a teacher at Dundee Community College, and when he visited Hilltown in 1952 he had taken a year's leave of his post to work on a project that had been dear to his heart for many years. His interest goes back to his own childhood, to his first day at primary school (1909), and his 'story' could only be told in the context of his life and his collaboration with his wife, Norah.

Norah and William Montgomerie

I was introduced to the work of Norah and William Montgomerie in the late 1960s when I was a post-graduate student in Folklore at Memorial University of Newfoundland. The founder of the department, Professor Herbert Halpert, was an inspiring teacher with an encyclopaedic knowledge of British Folklore. He would bring to class an armful of books 'you ought to know about' as well as fieldwork recordings to illustrate his lectures. Reel-to-reel tapes and 'records' played on huge machines were a regular feature — old 78 rpms, 7-inch 45s and 12-inch 33 rpms — and occasionally he would bring bright red acetate discs he had recorded during his own fieldwork in the 1930s. Among them were recordings he made in 1939 of children playing in the streets of New York. Though time and distance separated all the students from the rhymes and songs we heard in class, yet there was an instant familiarity to all of us. The universality and antiquity of childlore soon became evident as Halpert drew attention to versions of these rhymes in Scotland, collected by Robert Chambers and published in *Popular Rhymes of Scotland*, Edinburgh, 1826. For the twentieth century, Halpert highlighted the work of William and Norah Montgomerie published in 1946, *Scottish Nursery Rhymes,* as well as further collections. I confess now to a secret pride in my fellow Scots, and, having trained as a teacher, was interested in their motivation for collecting early childhood traditions. Although the main reference for Halpert's Childlore class was Iona and Peter Opie's *Lore and Language of School Children*, (Oxford, OUP, 1959), he noted that "The Montgomeries were the first in recent decades to stimulate interest in children's rhymes."[10]

In 1984, shortly after I joined the teaching and research staff of the School of Scottish Studies at the University of Edinburgh, my senior colleague Hamish Henderson introduced me to Norah and William (Bill) Montgomerie. In retirement (1973) they had moved from Dundee to Edinburgh, and, like Hamish, lived near the university. They liked to walk across The Meadows to the libraries or to attend public seminars and events, and were regular visitors to the School of Scottish Studies, where it was my good fortune to meet them. The 'Friday afternoon seminars' drew speakers from several departments, and in ensuing 'question-time, open to the floor', Bill Montgomerie (who had come to listen) was frequently brought into discussions as he had a profound knowledge of literature in several languages. He was renowned for his expertise in the classic ballad and had published articles about his research as well as on aspects of childlore.

Dr Francis Collinson, former music research fellow at The School of Scottish Studies, who reviewed Montgomerie's work in 1958 remarked that "Dr. William Montgomerie brings scholarship of a high order to bear on the problems of Scottish song, nursery rhyme and ballad ... he moves in a field not so far touched by the School of Scottish Studies..."[11] Over 25 years later, when part of my remit as a lecturer was to prepare and teach a new course in Childlore, the work of Norah and William Montgomerie was already familiar to me; getting to know them was a gift.

Outside of the university I met the Montgomeries at poetry readings, art exhibitions, concerts, ceilidhs, 'folk nights', theatre, storytelling events, and informal visits which nurtured a friendship that lasted till Bill died in 1994 and Norah in 1998. Over these years we shared countless cups of tea, and in 'writing their story' I am fortunate to be able to draw from discussions we had during those years. Bill himself showed me the recording machines he used (described above), and gave me cassette copies of some of his recordings, including the tape he made in the Dundee playground in 1952. Thanks to the School of Scottish Studies Archive, the original reel-to-reel tape has been digitised and can now be heard on CD as well as online.[12] Bill and Norah's daughter Dian Elvin has also been a great help, especially when I felt I was searching for a 'piece missing' from my jigsaw puzzle. I value her friendship as well as her emails and her essay, "William Montgomerie", published online by the Scottish Poetry Library.

Folklorists and Scots language activists

William and Norah Montgomerie began collecting children's rhymes, songs, chants and games in the 1930s, and in 1946 they published their first book, *Scottish Nursery Rhymes*. For 75 years their books have been favourites among parents, children and teachers, reprinted in many editions and also published in the USA, Canada, and Australia. Yet, apart from a few American folklorists — notably Alan Lomax, Herbert Halpert and Archer Taylor[13] — the Montgomeries themselves have seldom received the recognition they deserve. They formed a remarkable team, combining their interests, dedication and meticulous attention to detail and scholarship while recording and documenting the rhymes, chants, singing games and other playground lore.

The Montgomeries were interested in language acquisition and the importance of early childhood learning as a foundation for adult literacy and usage, particularly of Scots and all its dialects. They advised that "these rhymes should precede the pleasure derived from the more mature folksongs and ballads. Indeed, their fundamental quality attunes young ears to all poetry."[4]

Reflecting on his own experience of school in Glasgow at the age of five, Bill realised there was something amiss in an education system which banned the native speech of children, then challenged pupils to read and recite that language as it appeared in the poetry book used in the classroom – "Tam o Shanter" and "The Twa Corbies" were memorised, as were passages from Walter Scott and other 'greats'. As a student in Glasgow University in the early 1920s, he studied English Literature and became keenly aware that it was not his formal schooling that enabled him to appreciate ancient ballads or the fifteenth century Scots 'makars', but the language of his early childhood, at home and in the playground.

After graduation, Montgomerie trained as a school-teacher, and soon learned that every trainee teacher in Scotland was obliged to learn about the Scottish Education Act (1872). Based on the Elementary Education Act of 1870 (England and Wales), it had been passed to provide compulsory education *in the English language* for children aged 5 to 13. Forty years on, when I trained as a teacher in the mid-1960s, students were assessed by the Speech and Drama tutors, and remedial sessions were arranged for those who did not comply with the 'standard English' required for the classroom. Fellow students who were told they spoke in an 'overly' Glasgow or Ayrshire accent felt embarrassed at being singled out, and some from the Highlands and Islands were cautioned (even before they spoke) not to devoice 'd' to 't' and 'v' to 'f' for that would sound 'too Highland'. Such methods ensured that the Scottish Education Department would achieve its aim of strict adherence to the 1872 Act, and new teachers often resorted to meting out the same chastisement they had experienced. Generations of children were humiliated and punished for speaking in their mother tongue – Scots, Lallans, Doric, Gaelic or Norn – and too often their parents were the teachers' best allies. The languages were devalued, and Scots was labelled as 'nothing but bad grammar' or a debased form of 'good English', and any teacher who disagreed was not only a very rare exception to the rule but might also be advised to keep that opinion out of the classroom.[15]

William Montgomerie began his career in Dundee, teaching English at a secondary school (11 to 18 year-olds) before moving to 'higher education' to lecture at a community college. He resolved, however, to continue his collecting from oral tradition despite the lack of interest shown by colleagues in education. It might have been a lonely furrow to plough had it not been for the good fortune of meeting Norah Shargool, a young artist from London who worked with the Dundee newspaper empire of D.C. Thomson. Together they were to leave an enormous legacy which deserves recognition. In 'telling their story' and sharing examples of their collections, this book gives an insight into their lives and pays tribute to the Montgomeries, whose work is as important today as it was when they first began.

Bill and Norah: Biographical sketches

William Montgomerie, son of Rachel (Sinclair) and John Montgomerie, was born in Glasgow on May 30, 1904. He grew up in a strict, religious household as his father was a Plymouth Brethren evangelist who did not allow his children to attend secular events such as parties, or even bring friends to the house. His father worked as a painter and decorator, except during the 1914-18 War when, being a pacifist, he was imprisoned as a conscientious objector. His strictness at home was not a reflection of harshness, but of his deep religious convictions.[16] Among school-friends in neighbouring playgrounds and city streets, however, Bill enjoyed "a typical Glasgow schoolboy's life, free to roam and fight, albeit often against his father's orders".

He would explore the surrounding countryside, looking at wildlife and nature in all around him. He loved books on history and literature and developed his own skills in creative writing and poetry. Montgomerie did well at school, so went on to Glasgow University where he studied English Literature, German, Chemistry, and other subjects. As mentioned, he graduated as a teacher then moved to the industrial city of Dundee, once renowned for fleets of whaling vessels that docked there from the mid-1800s, and for jute, jam and journalism — the 'comic capital' of Scotland.

While still in his twenties, Montgomerie's first book of poetry, *Via*, was published in London, (by Boriswood, 1933) with a second collection the following year: *Squared Circle: a Vision of the Cairngorms*.[17] Among poets, he soon earned a reputation which lasted the rest of his life, gaining recognition from the likes of Hugh MacDiarmid, Maurice Lindsay, and Kenneth Rexroth, who included his work in their anthologies. At poetry readings in Scotland he appeared with Sorley Maclean, Norman MacCaig, and Hamish Henderson, who all shared literary interests that included traditional poetry, song, storytelling and folklore. Maclean and MacCaig were both schoolteachers, Henderson a university lecturer, and Montgomerie also earned his living as a teacher.

Whether appearing in public or in a small, informal group, Montgomerie generally seemed very serious, though always approachable and insightful. Norah usually accompanied him, and, whether seated in the audience or beside Bill in the company, she had a sunny disposition, smiled and laughed easily, and had bright, expressive eyes. Norah was a visual artist; she was very fond of poetry and also wrote poems, but didn't consider herself to be a poet. She loved traditional rhymes, songs and stories and expressed her appreciation of them in her hoppity-skippity drawings of children playing.

Norah's background could scarcely have been more different from Bill's austere upbringing. She was born in West Dulwich, London, on April 6, 1909, the daughter of Letitia [Collins], a tailoress and John Shargool, an accountant. She described her family background as being Scottish, with Irish, Indian and some Italian influences, and she grew up in a musical household where the children were encouraged to enjoy music and the arts. In the introduction to her compilation of play rhymes for infants and young children (1966), Norah wrote, "Play rhymes [were] a tradition in my family. My own first recollection is sharing and playing them with my great-grandmother..."[18].

As the First World War had started when Norah was of school age, her parents feared that London was in danger, so she was educated at a convent boarding school in Folkestone (Kent). On leaving school she worked in London as a freelance magazine illustrator to finance art school and prepare for a career as an artist.

In 1991, Norah, by then a family friend and well-known to the students studying Childlore,[19] agreed to be recorded during the following conversation[20]:

From childhood in London to a career in Dundee

Norah: I was the oldest of quite a large family, Catholic family, my great-grandmother lived with us until she died at the age of 95. [Her name was Clara Saunders Lewis] and she was very Scots, and I can remember going to my mother and saying, "I can speak Scots — *Ah ken!*" (laughs) When I was very young [my great-grandmother] used to take me for long walks. We lived in Herne Hill, in London, and went down to a large park, and I would push my doll's pram, and she had her paper, and I had my paper, *The Rainbow*. And I would get out my paper, and she would say, "Norah, you know you can't read!" And then she would come out with songs and so forth, and then she would think of nursery rhymes, you know. Although my great-grandmother hadn't a very Scottish voice, because she lived in London most of her life, the rhymes were from her own childhood, and she would sing them because I was interested.[21] Well, I always liked children ... and because I was interested in children, I tended to draw children more than adults — I really did love drawing children, and most of the freelance work I had done was for children's books, and so forth.

MB: You mentioned you were quite young when you came to Scotland — what made you come?

NM: I saw an advert in the *Daily Mirror* for an artist with DC Thompson ... a publisher, and I knew they did children's things, and I'd done some freelance work in London, so I took my portfolio to the office and got the job ... 1930, was it, in the studio of DC Thomson in Dundee. I arrived in Dundee and found that my address was, Mrs Scroggie, Blackness Avenue, Dundee, and the first thing I saw as I came out of the station was a tram with "Blackness" on it, so I thought, "Oh, well, [laughs], this doesn't sound very promising," you know. However, Mrs Scroggie was this very kindly, kind person, and I got a bedroom right at the very top of the house. Blackness Avenue runs from up the hills, practically to the top, and down the main road ... the houses were tenemented ... and there were a lot of students and young people there. [Until I moved to Dundee], the only pictures that I'd seen of Scotland were old paintings or photographs — black-and-white photographs, which were rather dreary, you know, and when I got out of the train was all this colour, you know, because you saw the hills, and the Blue Law Hill — there was a lot of colour everywhere!

MB: Reading your books about children's rhymes, what struck me was how intently you must have listened ... not only to children playing and reciting rhymes, but also to their mothers, singing and talking to the children. When did you get interested in that?

NM: I got to know one or two elderly neighbours, and so forth, and I got them interested in rhymes, which they thought was just nonsense. Well, eventually I started writing them down ... in a notebook or bits of paper, but a notebook really, and I didn't feel strange with Scots because of my great-grandmother. ... When I came to Dundee, the sound of people speaking seemed quite familiar, you know ... my great-grandmother, she would come out with songs and so forth, and then she would think of nursery rhymes you know.

Meeting Bill

MB: You now have a huge collection that both you and Bill have worked on and put into your books .... Did you meet Bill in Dundee?

NM: I did indeed, and it's rather a strange story, because I had a boyfriend in London who was Austrian, and so one of the things I was determined to do was to learn German. And I found there was a German club in Dundee, and it was run by William Montgomerie ... So that's how I got to know him, and then, in my digs I was with a German lady in Dundee, who had married a Scotsman, and so, curiously enough, that was how I got to know Bill — it was because I was interested in German.

MB: Had Bill moved [from Glasgow] to Dundee to teach German?

NM: He wasn't teaching German at all — his subject is English, English literature. So, he was teaching English.

MB: You had many, many more other interests in common as well — song collecting, and everything else.

NM: Well, mainly I would say walking ... we lived in a very interesting part of Scotland that not many people really bothered about. Dundee is on the edge, it's near fishing villages like Arbroath and Authmithie, and it's also only about 5 miles from a number of glens.... Strathmore was just behind Dundee, and after Strathmore there were all these glens. We were both very keen on walking. I remember my first weekend living there, I walked from Dundee to Kirriemuir, [the distance there and back is 32 miles]. I wanted to do it because Kirriemuir is the birthplace of J. M. Barrie, who wrote Peter Pan, and of course I love Peter Pan.

MB: So, walking has been part of your lives all those years, not only in Scotland but far beyond — Bill showed me his walking stick with all the badges on it from places all over Europe, places that you've walked together.

NM: When he found I was interested in Germany we went to Germany together with the Scottish Youth Hostel Association...

Collaborating and Collecting

Norah's notebooks benefited from Bill's input as he helped with dialect words, phrases, and other aspects of collecting. In 1934 Norah and Bill were married and made their home in Broughty Ferry, on the outskirts of the city. They had two children, Dian born in 1935 and Iain in 1940, who both became artists.

MB: How long were you collecting before you decided to publish a book?

NM: Well, I suppose about five years, you know, gradually (we gathered the collection). At first I just listened to them, and then I started to write them down, and I had a neighbour was very good, and she corrected the spelling and so forth, and I also wrote down the tunes, because a lot of them had tunes, but the tunes have been dropped from the latest edition ... I don't know why – publishers are not very keen on publishing music ... Perhaps a cassette is the answer. That's much better than writing them down ... I have made a sort of collection of singing games, with the tunes ...

MB: So this collection, was it before the war when you started?

NM: Oh yes, yes! It was from when I began living in Dundee [1930]. Well, when we had all this book gathered together [and approached publishers], and nobody was interested you know. So, I sent some of them to – you'll be amazed – Walter de la Mare.[22] And "Yes", he said. "Oh, these are lovely! They make my one little drop of Scottish blood dance!" So that was very kind of him, and he put me in touch with someone in Hogarth Press ... in 1942, I think ... and it was Hogarth Press published it (in 1946).

Though frustrating and disappointing that no Scottish publisher would consider their manuscript, it may not be surprising that Hogarth Press picked up on Walter de la Mare's introduction of a fellow poet, for Hogarth Press was run by two poets: Leonard Woolf and John Lehmann.[23] It was a stroke of ingenuity on Norah's part, and the publication not only encouraged the Montgomeries to continue, but the book also caught the attention of reviewers on both sides of the Atlantic.

Audio-recording the voices of tradition

Bill and Norah dedicated their first book to their two children, then aged eleven and five. Dian recalled her father's fieldwork which, as already mentioned, became a prominent feature of their family weekends and holidays.

NM: Bill recorded on a funny little machine called a Wirex...

MB: What year would that have been?

NM: That would have been just before – or was it just after? – the war ... I wasn't very interested or knowledgeable about the actual machine.... How it worked [thin steel wire was pulled across the recording head of the machine, pre-dating the use of acetate tape used in tape-recorders.]

MB: And it was powered by battery, or electricity?

NM: Oh, battery. Nothing ran by electricity in those days ... I mean, it was just so he could make the collection ... It was far less organised than it is now [in established archives] ... There was no money at all ... that didn't come into it really – it was the feeling that Scotland had so many songs, not only songs, but stories that were so [worthwhile] – you know, people lived alone up in the hills ... they made their own entertainment ...

MB: Bill told me he used to cycle – did you go with him [cycling] when he collected?

NM: No, I scarcely ever did, because by this time I had a small child, a small daughter, a baby – Dian. And that was followed by a small son, who was born just at the beginning of the war... they kept me busy, but I was very interested ... but in no way could I go cycling — I did have a bike... but a very ancient one; it was one that a friend had given me and that was almost tied together with bits of elastic and things like that, but it worked. (laughter) But it didn't work well enough to go on long trips with Bill.

MB: And did Bill used to take the Wirex on his bike?

NM: Yes, of course. It wasn't very large, if I remember rightly it was about this size: [Norah demonstrates with her hands c. 18 inches].

MB: Yes, and what about the newer kind of machinery... the tape recorder — when did these recordings appear?

NM: Oh, well that was during the war, I think, when tape recorders appeared. [Norah takes Margaret to see Bill's collection] and then this one, this cumbersome — [she points to a large, reel-to-reel machine].

MB: That's a Ferrograph.

NM: Well, the Ferrograph seemed one of the best machines to get hold of.

MB: Yes. We've listened to the recordings, and they are remarkable. Is that the same machine that he's had since the 50s?

NM: Yes, it is.

MB: Surely, Bill, you didn't take that one on your bike? This machine is very large and heavy.

BM: No.

NM: No, darling, you didn't. We didn't have a car until, well, it must have been just after the war. So, I'm not quite sure how we, how you managed that —

MB: Bill, you went to Arbroath and recorded people there, and Auchmithie?

BM: Yes.

MB: And you recorded children in schools, too, didn't you Bill? [Bill acknowledges with a nod.]

NM: Well, yes that was in Hilltown school that you went to.

BM: Yes, Hilltown.

NM: It was called Hilltown... And I'm afraid that the headmaster wasn't very interested, he said, "Oh, I don't think, you know, that they do that [sing] — well, perhaps they do sing these songs ..." But I mean so many people thought that nursery rhymes and these children's songs were just a lot of nonsense.

Visiting a playground in Dundee

In June 1952 Bill took his Ferrograph to Hilltown, Dundee, where he recorded nearly 50 items of 'nonsense' sung by a group of children in a school playground. The tapes, now deposited in the School of Scottish Studies Archive, also record 22 songs and ballads from elderly farm-workers in rural areas, and four ballads sung by fellow-poet Norman MacCaig.[24] The range of the collection represents the main areas of Montgomerie's interests, and though colleagues in education were dubious about the worth of studying childlore, his studies of traditional ballads and related manuscripts (such as the lists of Scots words and phrases Bill and Norah collected) were of great interest to two professors of literature, language and linguistics at the University of Edinburgh: Angus McIntosh[25] and William L. Renwick.[26] Following their advice, Montgomerie began to work on a PhD, and in 1952 had taken leave of his teaching job to complete the research and write his thesis on Scottish ballad manuscripts.[27] He had made an intensive study of all the manuscripts consulted by Frances James Child, and noted the absence of versions written down from oral tradition and also ballad versions sung by children: "[Child] was too limited by his conception of traditional ballads as poems whose nature could most accurately be apprehended in manuscript form.... But there are other things in the ballad MSS. ... They contain singing games and nursery rhymes."[28] He and Norah had already written down versions of Child ballads, which they published in their first book; among them were 'The Croodlin Doo' (a version of 'Lord Randal', Child 12) and 'The False Knight' (Child 3), but only a 'live recording' would demonstrate that they were still part of Scotland's oral tradition. William Montgomerie was to prove the point in the recordings he made in Hilltown, Dundee, when a fourteen-year-old boy sang a version of 'The Cruel Mother' (Child 20) – 'Poor Lady Lido'.

Montgomerie completed the PhD in 1953 and returned to his role as a teacher. It must have been a bitter disappointment to him, however, that after submitting his manuscript he was no longer required by the university, and his 'year out' also affected his job. Looking back on her father's life, Dian writes: "Dundee Education Authority disapproved of his spending a year, on a very small grant, writing up his doctoral thesis, and demoted him."[29]

Using the Scots Language in the playground and in print

Apart from a few ditties published in a 2-page article, "Skipping and stotting rhymes from the bairns of Dundee and Angus, collected by William and Norah Montgomerie", the tape-recorded collection has never been published. The rhymes were included in the literary journal, *Chapman*, which had already published some of William Montgomerie's own poems and would later devote two issues to his work. In keeping with the style of the literary journal, the rhymes and poems stand alone, without annotation or translation.[30] William and Norah Montgomerie's books of nursery rhymes, however, have a glossary under the title of 'Words you may not know', as one of the aims of publishing their collections was to keep alive the 'native tongue' of the folk who recited them.

The Montgomeries not only recognised the importance of pre-school years in language acquisition, but also of having fun and enjoyment. On the pages of their books, small children would meet birds and animals, 'creepy crawlies' and 'wee beasties' that jumped and danced, spoke, and made you laugh. Soon they would recognise them in the world about them: the gowk (cuckoo), hoggie (sheep), moudiewort (mole), Coorie Ann (wren), deuk (duck), corbie (carrion crow), gled (buzzard), heatherbleat (snipe), laverock (lark), merle (blackbird), papingoe (parrot), pyot (magpie), hurcheon (hedgehog), kye (cattle), ousen (oxen), yowe (ewe), tod (fox), whitterit (weasel), and wul-cat (wild cat).[31] As there would be no provision for the language in the school curriculum, young children who already understood Scots would hopefully use it at home and in the playground.[32]

In introducing their first book, the Montgomeries wrote a letter to the nursery rhymes, rather than a preface or introduction to the readers[33]:

Dear Scottish Nursery Rhymes,

You have been flying about Scotland for hundreds of years. Some of you have been as elusive as the golden eagle, as inaccessible as the ptarmigan. Mr Robert Chambers, over a hundred years ago, collected many of you in his aviary. But for him you might have died out altogether like our capercaillie, and much of our early poetry. It is a pity that his aviary looked rather like a museum of stuffed birds with Latin names, and that children were not invited. *Lagopus mutus* in a glass case, on Sunday afternoon, is a poor thing compared with the white ptarmigan snoring over the grey lichened rocks in the Cairngorms, heard only by the mountaineer.

We hope to see your corbies and laverocks as welcome in the British Nursery as English Mother Goose and the four and twenty blackbirds. You will migrate, and dance in the minds and feet of children who have never seen Scotland, but will know of the country through you. You may travel across the Atlantic to America, or down under to Australia and New Zealand, where there are folk who once knew you and will welcome you. You are ambassadors.

Children who know you will grow up to love Scottish ballads and songs, and then William Dunbar and Robert Henryson will not seem strange. Robert Burns, William Souter's *Seeds in the Wind*,[34] and Hugh McDiarmid's *Sangshaw*[35] will seem familiar country.

Norah and William Montgomerie

The corbies and laverocks had already travelled the Atlantic and beyond, and so did their books, thanks to publishers in New York, Toronto and Sydney. Their work provided comparative texts and tunes for overseas scholars, particularly eminent American folklorists such as Herbert Halpert and Archer Taylor[36] as well as ballad specialists Bernard H. Bronson[37], Emily Lyle[38], James Porter, Herschel Gower[39] and William B. McCarthy.[40] The 'critters' too were familiar to folk overseas who sensed a kinship, having 'met them' — or ones very like them — in their own region.

It was to take nearly four decades before *Scottish Nursery Rhymes* appeared under a Scottish imprint, appropriately W & R Chambers of Edinburgh (1985). Bill was 81 and Norah 76, and, having lost none of their dedication, they wrote in the Introduction to *Chambers Traditional Scottish Nursery Rhymes*:

> Our first two collections were published during the war and in the post-war years, since when the tide of Scottish language has ebbed further and left these sea-shells lying higher up the beach. But, like the sea urchins, we picked up on a Scottish shore, and still look at them with pleasure, they have lost none of their fascination. They should be shared with new generations of children whose heritage they are.[41]

The Montgomeries published many books, mostly together, but also individually, and Bill's output was also in demand for scholarly journals and poetry collections. The books listed (at the end)were written for children and their parents or adult companions, and covered a much wider range of tradition than represented on the Hillstreet recording. Their children's books included counting-out rhymes, riddles, tongue-twisters, finger-play and other 'baby-lore', weather-lore, place-lore, and folktales and legends. Additional information, usually on the dust jacket or back cover, reminded adult readers of the benefit of sharing the rhymes with their children, such as this note, published in 1990: "The transition from these rhymes, many of which are the words of folk songs, to adult folksongs of the folk clubs, and from them to the classic ballads, is a natural progression."[42]

Having gained the confidence of publishing companies, however, it seemed that bending an ear at the Scottish Education Department was out of the question, not only for the Montgomeries but also an ever-widening 'circle' dismayed at the language policy followed in Scottish schools — for example, under the heading of 'War poetry', pupils would study Wilfred Owen and Rupert Brooks — undoubtedly fine poets — yet there would be no poems in Scots, such as 'Epitaph' by William Montgomerie[43] or any by his fellow-folklorist, Hamish Henderson, whose war poems, *Elegies for the Dead in Cyrenaica*, were awarded the prestigious Somerset Maughan prize for poetry in 1947. It may have been celebrated in Cambridge by the likes of E.P. Thompson but it did not impress the Scottish Education Department, as the next generation, the 'baby boomers' would be schooled under the same guidelines. Like Montgomerie and Henderson, however, many would hold to the 'mither tongue', among them writer and language activist Billy Kay (b. 1951)[44]: the co-founder of *Chapman*, poet Walter Perrie (b. 1949), and subsequent editor, writer and literary critic Joy Hendry (b. 1953).

Poets and writers of all generations enjoyed a vibrant literary scene in Edinburgh, which suited the Montgomeries in their retirement. From 1977 to 1984 William Montgomerie was editor of the poetry magazine *Lines Review*,[45] and, with Norah, continued to work on literary and folklore projects until health began to decline. When Bill and Norah died they left a treasure-trove of manuscripts, with several 'works in progress' including Norah's retelling of the legends of the Celtic hero, Finn MacCoul, whose exploits link Ireland and Scotland. It would be pleasing to Norah and Bill that the manuscript was edited by their grandson, Julian Brooks, and her proposed book, *The Fantastical Feats of Finn MacCoul* was published in Edinburgh in 2009.

The Montgomeries' devotion to folklore and language never faltered, and neither did their hopes for recognition of 'the mither tongue'. Almost seventy years after the publication of *Scottish Nursery Rhymes,* the Scottish government department 'Education Scotland' (replacing the former Scottish Education Department), launched their Scots Language Policy in 2015, to "recognise the important role that school education has in promoting the use of Scots". The curriculum underwent many stages of development and now aims to "promote the acquisition, use and development of Scots in education, media, publishing and the arts".[46]

The material gathered by the Montgomeries over many decades is as relevant today as it was when they first collected it, "not merely" as Grainger wrote, to conserve "the tunes and words ... but [also to] give an enduring picture of the lives, art and traditions ... dialects ... and other personal characteristics of singers."

The voices of the Hilltown children recorded in 1952 reflect the joy of singing, playing, laughing and having fun — the bairns in the playground had no need to analyse their hand-eye co-ordination, speed of movement, agility, flexibility, accuracy of pronunciation, rhythm or tempo, or the process of memorising text. They had no need to worry about being silly, inhibited, or about keeping fit; they have a lot to teach us.

And so, to the Dundee playground in the 'Hilltoon' where these rhymes, songs and games were recorded.

NOTES

1 Grainger, Percy. 'Collecting with the Phonograph' *Journal of the Folk-Song Society*, Vol. 3, No. 12 (May, 1908), pp. 147-162. The same journal also has transcriptions of the songs recorded by Grainger: see Lucy E. Broadwood, Percy Grainger, Cecil J. Sharp, Ralph Vaughan Williams, Frank Kidson, J. A. Fuller-Maitland, and A. G. Gilchrist. "Songs Collected by Percy Grainger", *Journal of the Folk-Song Society*, vol. 3, no. 12, 1908, pp. 170–242. *JSTOR*, <www.jstor.org/stable/4433927>. Accessed 21 Nov. 2020.

2 Over 200 of Grainger's wax cylinders survive and are archived in the Archive of Folk Song in the Library of Congress. Grainger emigrated to America in 1914 and spent the rest of his life there.

3 Quoted by Michael Yates in 'Percy Grainger and the Impact of the Phonograph' p. 267 in *Folk Music Journal*, Vol. 4, No. 3 (1982), pp. 265-275. Yates examined the correspondence between members of the Folk-Song Society, which is now archived at the Vaughan Williams Memorial Library. See also discussion by Graham Freeman, "'That Chief Undercurrent of My Mind': Percy Grainger and the Aesthetics of English Folk Song." *Folk Music Journal*, vol. 9, no. 4, 2009, pp. 581–617.

4 Having visited Eriskay in 1905, Marjorie Kennedy Fraser was captivated by the Gaelic songs she heard, and was keen to record as many as possible lest they be lost. Her published works with Kenneth MacLeod (translator) fulfilled a parallel aim of arranging the songs for the concert platform. *Songs of the Hebrides and Other Celtic Songs from The Highlands of Scotland*, 3 Vols., London: Boosey & Hawkes, 1909–1921.

5 He recorded several hundred songs on wax cylinder before returning to the United States, where he hoped to publish his remarkable

collection. See Ian A. Olson, "Scottish Song in the James Madison Carpenter Collection." *Folk Music Journal*, vol. 7, no. 4, 1998, pp. 421–433 and Julia C. Bishop, "'Dr Carpenter from the Harvard College in America': An Introduction to James Madison Carpenter and His Collection." *Folk Music Journal*, vol. 7, no. 4, 1998, pp. 402–420.

6   Together and individually, the Campbells left a remarkable collection of recordings as well as publications. A selection of audio recordings can be heard via *Tobar an Dualchais/ Kist of Riches*

7   See Campbell, John Lorne, and Hugh Cheape. *A Very Civil People : Hebridean Folk, History and Tradition*. Edinburgh: Birlinn, 2000. In his introduction, Hugh Cheape summarises the chronology of Campbell's use of audio-recording devices, pp. x–xiii.

8   I am grateful to Dian Montgomerie Elvin for her sharing her memories, by email, telephone and also via her biographic summary of her father's life, published by the Scottish Poetry Library. See ‹https://www.scottishpoetrylibrary.org.uk/poet/william-montgomerie/x›

9   Discussion with Lesley McLuckie is quoted from a 'Zoom' recording (Nov. 2020) and follow-up emails.

10 Despite the wide geographic spread of the Opies' fieldwork, their comprehensive bibliography, *The Lore and Language of Schoolchildren* makes no mention of earlier books by William and Norah Montgomerie. Without the benefit of the internet that now makes it easy to connect, it seemed possible that they had not seen the books or met the Montgomeries during trips to Scotland. Dian remembers their visits, however, recalling that they were friends of her parents, which is confirmed in the Montgomeries' second book, *Sandy Candy*, published in 1948, in which they thank (among others) Mrs Iona Opie (p. 7), who, by then, they had met. As the omission of the Montgomerie books is repeated in Sylvia Ann Grider's scholarly article, "A Select Bibliography of Childlore" *Western Folklore*,

39, no. 3, (1980), pp. 248–265, Halpert made a point of noting the significance of their work in a follow-up article, "Childlore Bibliography: A Supplement" *Western Folklore*, 41, no. 3 (1982), pp. 205-28.

11 Francis Collinson, "Reviewed Works: *'The Twa Corbies', 'Sir Walter Scott as Ballad Editor', 'William Motherwell and Robert A. Smith'* by William Montgomerie; *Some Notes on the Herd Manuscripts* by William Montgomerie" in *Journal of the English Folk Dance and Song Society*, vol. 8, no. 3, 1958, p. 170. *JSTOR*, <www.jstor.org/stable/4521565>. Accessed March 11, 2020

12 The University of Edinburgh website: <www.tobarandualchais.co.uk>

13 In a review of their first book, Folklore Professor Archer Taylor highly commends the work of the Montgomeries to ballad scholars as well as those interested in childlore. Alan Lomax, who visited Scotland in 1951, noted that William Montgomerie was one of four collector-folklorists who assisted him during his monumental recording project for the Columbia World Library of Folk and Primitive Music. The LP sleeve notes: "Edited by Alan Lomax, with the MacLeans of Raasay, Hamish Henderson and William Montgomerie". Lomax fellow-folklorist Herbert Halpert had been recording folksongs and childlore since the mid-1930s, when they were part of a Work Projects Administration (WPA) project, set up by the Federal Government during the depression. Halpert wrote his post-grad M.A. thesis on "Folk Rhymes of New York City Children" (Columbia University, 1946). See also H. Halpert, "Childlore Bibliography: A Supplement." *Western Folklore* vol. 41, no. 3 (1982): pp. 205-28.

14 *Traditional Scottish Nursery Rhymes* (1995), p. 7.

15 In Wales, as in Gaelic Scotland, the Act had a particularly negative effect on the health of the Welsh language. According to a research article, 'WELSH: The Welsh language in education in the UK'.

"[T]his act is widely believed to be one of the most damaging pieces of legislation in the social history of the Welsh language, as hundreds of thousands of children in Wales who very often knew no English were taught in English only. Tactics which would today be known as emotional and physical abuse were used in order to ensure that children did not use their first and very often only language."
<https://www.mercator-research.eu/fileadmin/mercator/documents/regional_dossiers/welsh_in_the_uk_2ᵈ.pdf>

16 Two of Montgomerie's poems, 'Ma Faither' and 'Breaking of Bread' reflect the influence of his hard-working, fun-loving, deeply religious, and Scots-speaking father. See William Montgomerie, *From Time to Time: Selected Poems*, Edinburgh (Canongate), 1985, pp. 5–13.

17 Several of his poems had already been published in literary magazines and journals including *John O'London's Weekly*, *The Adelphi*, *The Scots Magazine*, and *The Scottish Educational Journal*.

18 Norah Montgomerie (compiler), *This Little Pig Went to Market: Play Rhymes for Infants and Young Children*, London, Sydney, Toronto (The Bodley Head), 1966, new edition, 1983, p.11.

19 From the mid-1980s to mid-90s, the University offered a course in Childlore as part of the newly established degree, later labelled Scottish Ethnology. The Gaelic section of the course in Childlore was taught by Dr Alan Bruford (1937–95) while I taught the section devoted to Scots traditions. Norah was especially interested to attend, as she was keen to discover what young folk sang, played, and remembered from the school playgrounds of the 1970s to 90s. Students valued the opportunity to get to know her, recognising the importance of the Montgomeries' work to the wider scholarship of Folklore. Among the students were Leila Dudley Edwards and Elizabeth Carnegie, who both followed careers in Folklore. The course no longer exists.

20   The original plan was to record both Norah and Bill, but sadly that was not to be, as Bill was suddenly admitted to hospital, seriously ill. When he returned home, alas he was not able to take part, though he was totally engaged as an observer while Norah told their story. The tape-recording can be accessed at the School of Scottish Studies Archive, SA1991.102, with thanks to Leila Dudley Edwards who transcribed the original.

21   Similarly, folklorist Anne Geddes Gilchrist (1863–1954), born and brought up in Lancashire, attributed her interest to the fact that she was "a full blooded Scot on both sides of her family". Lyn A. Wolz. "Resources in the Vaughan Williams Memorial Library: The Anne Geddes Gilchrist Manuscript Collection." *Folk Music Journal*, vol. 8, no. 5, 2005, pp. 619–639. *JSTOR*, <www.jstor.org/stable/4522748>. Accessed February 27, 2020. The Montgomeries corresponded with Anne Geddes Gilchrist, who wrote 11 letters to Bill (concerning the ballad) between 1948 and 1952. See the manuscript collection of the National Library of Scotland: <http://manuscripts.nls.uk/repositories/2/resources/10370>

22   Walter de la Mare (1873–1956), best remembered for his stories for children and poems such as 'The Listeners', is a long-time favourite.

23   Hogarth Press was founded in 1917 by Leonard and Virginia Woolf and in 1938 she relinquished her interest in the business which was then run in partnership with John Lehmann.

24   The tape-recording accession numbers range between SA 1952.044 and SA 1952.054. Most can be accessed on Tobar an Dualchais/Kist of Riches. See <http://tobarandualchais.co.uk/en/advancedsearch?page=8>

25   In 1948, Professor Angus McIntosh was appointed the first Forbes Professor of English Language and General Linguistics at the University of Edinburgh. From 1949 he was closely involved in the

planning and administration of the Linguistic Survey of Scotland, an ambitious project documenting all the Scots dialects. McIntosh was also one of the prime movers in the founding of the School of Scottish Studies at the University of Edinburgh in 1951.

26　In 1945 Professor Renwick was appointed Regis Professor of Rhetoric and English Literature at the University of Edinburgh, and until 1951 collaborated with Professor A. McIntosh in founding the School of Scottish Studies.

27　See Dian Montgomerie Elvin, online essay, Scottish Poetry Library.

28　William Montgomerie. "Bibliography of the Scottish Ballad Manuscripts, 1730-1825" unpublished PhD dissertation, 1953, The University of Edinburgh. Preface, pp, xxi–xxii.

29　Dian Montgomerie Elvin, online essay, Scottish Poetry Library.

30　*Chapman 23-24: Scots Language and Literature double issue*, Editor Joy Hendry, v. 5, nos. 5-6 (1979), p.76.

31　These appear in *Scottish Nursery Rhymes* (1946) and *Sandy Candy and other Scottish Nursery Rhymes* (1948)

32　Within the Scottish Education Department, little had changed half a century later when in 1997 David Purves wrote: "At school, a policy of cultural repression became the norm and generations of children were presented with an image of "correct" or "good" English, but little or no attempt was made to present an image of good Scots. Commonly, the natural speech of Scots children was simply represented as a deviation from good English." David Purves, *Scots Grammar: Scots Grammar and Usage*. Edinburgh, The Saltire Society. 1997, Revised Edition 2002, p. 2.

33　*Scottish Nursery Rhymes*, London, Hogarth Press, 1946, p. 6.

34   Dian Montgomerie recalls going to Perth with her parents to visit her father's friend and fellow-poet, William Soutar (1898–1943). At a young age she was familiar with Soutar's book, *Seeds in the Wind. Poems in Scots for Children*, first published in 1933 (Edinburgh), and in 2014 Dian produced an online translation of all the poems in the book. See <https://williamsoutar.com/Seeds%20in%20the%20Wind%20v1.pdf>

35   MacDiarmid's collection of poems, *Sangshaw*, has, for example, 'The Bonnie Broukit Bairn' (The beautiful neglected child) which ends with the oft-quoted phrase, 'the *haill clanjamfrie*' (*the whole lot, all of them*). *A recitation of it can be heard on* https://www.youtube.com/watch?v=2hov8wXCKnk. Montgomerie's letters from MacDiarmid, dating from 1932, are in the collections of the National Library of Scotland; see <http://manuscripts.nls.uk/repositories/2/resources/11579>

36   In his review of *Scottish Nursery Rhymes*, Taylor noted (1949) that the book "is now in its third impression and fully deserves this success …. it makes valuable additions to our stock of traditional rhymes and should stimulate study of them." See Archer, Taylor, *The Journal of American Folklore*, vol. 62, no. 244, 1949, pp. 214–214. *JSTOR*, <www.jstor.org/stable/536333. Accessed 11 Mar. 2020>.

37   *The Traditional Tunes of the Child Ballads, Volume 1*. Princeton University Press, 1959. (Acknowledgements).

38   Honorary Research Fellow at the University of Edinburgh, Dr Emily Lyle is internationally known for her ballad scholarship. She acknowledges the "pioneering bibliographical work done by Dr William Montgomerie" as a primary source for her work. See, Lyle, E.B., Crawfurd, A. & Scottish Text Society, 1975. *Andrew Crawfurd's Collection of Ballads and Songs*, Edinburgh: Scottish Text Society, p. 9.

39 *Jeannie Robertson: Emergent Singer, Transformative Voice,* Knoxville: University of Tennessee Press, 1995. (see pp. 115 – 127)

40 *The Ballad Matrix : Personality, Milieu, and the Oral Tradition.* Bloomington: Indiana University Press, 1990. (p. 52)

41 Introduction to *Scottish Nursery Rhymes,* selected and edited by Norah and William Montgomerie Edinburgh, Chambers, 1985 & 1990, p. 2.

42 *Chambers Traditional Scottish Nursery Rhymes.* p. 2.

43 *From Time to Time: selected poems,* Edinburgh: Canongate, 1985, p. 82.

44 Billy Kay's book, *Scots: The Mither Tongue* (Mainstream, 1986) became a best-seller and his work has been the basis for several radio and television programmes. See ‹http://www.billykay.co.uk/Pages/OdysseyProductions2.asp›

45 *Lines Review* was a Scottish poetry journal, founded in 1952 by Edinburgh publisher Callum Macdonald. The last edition, edited by poet Tessa Ransford, was published in 1998.

46 See ‹https://education.gov.scot/education-scotland/news-and-events/keeping-the-mither-tongue-alive-celebrating-minority-languages-in-all-their-diversity-and-distinctiveness/›

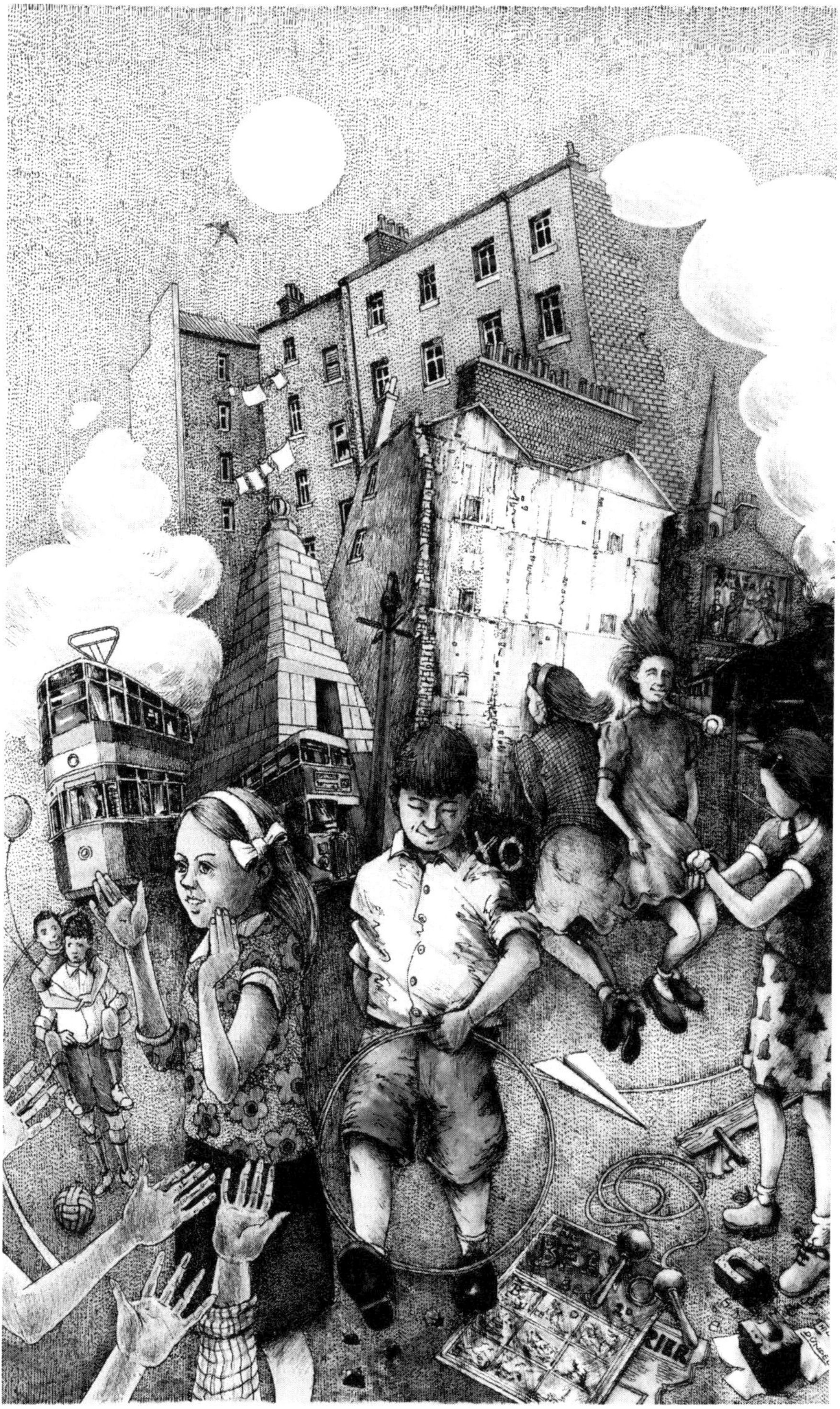

STREET SONGS, RHYMES AND GAMES

On the 24th of June 1952 Bill Montgomerie arrived at the school in Hilltown Dundee, carrying his Ferrograph reel-to-reel tape recorder, a microphone and a few reel-to-reel tapes. Being a teacher himself, he had requested permission to record the children, and though it was granted Norah recalled that "the headmaster wasn't very interested; he said, 'I don't think [the pupils in the school] sing these songs ...' So many people thought that these children's songs were just a lot of nonsense."[1] The children themselves welcomed the opportunity to sing, play and have fun, and during the session provided over 40 items which Bill recorded on three reel-to-reel tapes.[2] The songs, rhymes, chants and games recorded were not only a delight to the Montgomeries, but also represent Dundee's vibrant culture as well as the tenacity of oral tradition.

Almost seventy years have passed since the Hilltoon bairns sang these songs in the streets, playgrounds and 'courties' of Dundee. In school they had been taught to 'write correct English' and 'speak properly', but outside of the classroom there was freedom to use their ain toung. As Bill and Norah knew, the children were the laughing, singing, chanting, jumping, dancing, hopping, skipping, leaping, ball-bouncing, twirling custodians of the language of generations of mill-workers, paper-makers, printers, shipwrights, domestic servants, whalers, laundry maids and navvies. They lived in a colourful world, and, as Dundee poet Matthew Fitt explained in 2019 when asked about the way he wrote and spoke, 'Scots is meh mither tongue. Eh write in Scots because it's in meh haid and hert and is the best wey eh ken tae express meh view o the warld.'[3]

As the printed page cannot capture the music of the words or the speakers, the sound of the language is all-important. To Norah and Bill, it seemed that Scotland was slow to recognize this, so in 1955, when Columbia Records released a 12-inch LP of Alan Lomax's Scottish recordings, were encouraged by Lomax's inclusion of children singing. They hoped that a Scottish company would follow suit, and when cassette tapes had become more common than LPs, Norah was especially hopeful: "Perhaps a cassette is the answer." In 1985 there was a welcome breakthrough when Canongate Publishers introduced the Whigmaleerie Series of audio-books for children. They included selections from several Montgomerie books, but the producers decided it would be better to use the voices of popular Scottish actors, Mary Riggans from Clydebank (known for her role in 'Take the High Road' and the film' Balamory') and Sheila Donald from Leith (known for her role in 'The Steamie'). Similarly, while some of the songs in this collection have been featured on records (LP's), audio-cassettes and CDs, most are sung by adults, arranged with vocal harmonies and instrumental accompaniments. As entertainment they are widely enjoyed and have played an important role in teaching the songs to new generations.

The stars of stages, screens, concert platforms and folk-clubs have an important role to play in sustaining culture, but so also do the children in the playground and the street. Bill Montgomerie's recordings provide a unique opportunity to hear the voices of Dundee children, and the following pages provide a 'Song Book' of their words.

NOTES

1. Recorded conversation, School of Scottish Studies Archive, SA1991.102

2. Bill later donated his tapes to the newly established Archive of the School of Scottish Studies at the University of Edinburgh. The shelf numbers date the recording and the full accession numbers label individual items, which are listed here with each item. The recordings of the Hilltown children are on tapes SA1952/44, SA1952/45 and SA1952/46, and most of the tracks can be accessed online via the School of Scottish Studies Archive website, Tobar an Dualchais/Kist o Riches, <http://www.tobarandualchais.co.uk/>

3. Winner of the 2019 Scots Language Award: <https://projects.handsupfortrad.scot/scotslanguageawards/scots-language-awards-2019-matthew-fitt/?lang=en>

4. Recorded, SA1991/102.

5. The Whigmaleerie cassettes included 'Scottish Nursery Rhymes' and the traditional tale, 'White Pet' (selected from *The Well at the World's End: The Folktales of Scotland*.)

SINGING GAMES & ACTION SONGS

Errata

Page 39ff

2 ALL THE BOYS IN OUR TOWN. Line 5 in both verses: he cuddled her and sat her on his knee. Line 6: [and] said "Oh Darling, I love thee."

5. THE HOKEY POKEY. Line 6 both verses: around, not about. Shout after "That's what it's all about": "See!" Not "Woooo!"

7. BANKS O ABERFELDY. Verse 2, line 4: Ye'll get your licks the moarn. Verse 4: Yes, ma dearie, you may go. Verse 5: Off you go. Verse 7, line 2: We saw, we saw; Verse 9, line 2: We got, we got.

8. THERE CAME THREE DUKES. Verse 4: Marry one of us, sir etc Verse 6: Bend as well as you, sir etc. Verse 8: Just as clean as you, sir, etc. Final verse [girls singing]: Hop around the parlour, the parlour, the parlour, Hop around the parlour, Push one out.

29. TENSY, NINESY. Line 4: Twosy, stot the ball for onesy.

30. I'M THE MONSTER OF BLACKNESS. Line 2: My name you'll never guess

33: THE LONDON BALL. Line 4 of chorus: Please choose your partner.

34. ARE YOU GOING TO GOLF: Line 5: Up at the North Pole, sir. Line 7: Catching polar bears, sir.

35. CHARLIE CHAPLIN. Line 2: To show the ladies how to dance

37. ALLA BALLA AND THE FORTY THIEVES. Line 1: Ali Balla. Line 4: Alla Balla

42. MARY, QUEEN OF SCOTS. Lines 1 & 3: Mary Queen of Scots got her head chopped off

43. KNAVES AND SHEPHERDS. LINE 2: Knaves and shepherds come, come, come away.

SINGING GAMES & ACTION SONGS

1. Queen Mary, Queen Mary, my age is sixteen

Queen Mary, Queen Mary, my age is sixteen
My father's a farmer in yonder green
He's plenty o money to dress me in silk
But there's nae bonnie laddie'll tak me awa.

    Na, na, tattie man, na, na, tattie man
    There's nae bonnie laddie'll tak me awa.

This morning I and I looked in the glass
I said to mysel what a bonnie wee lass.
My hands by my side an I gave a 'Ha! Ha!'
There's nae bonnie laddie'll tak me awa

  Na, na, tattie man, na, na, tattie man
  There's nae bonnie laddie'll tak me awa.

One mornin I rose an I had a wee son
I sent for the doctor, the minister come;
He christened my baby an gave it name
His name was — Paddy McGraw

  Na, na, tattie man, na, na, tattie man
    There's nae bonnie laddie'll tak me awa.

2. All the boys in our town

All the boys in our town lead a happy life,
All except George — he wants a wife.
Oh, a wife he shall have, a girl of his own,
And that'll be Mrs — sitting on the throne.
[faster] Oh he kissed her and he cuddled her underneath the tree
They went down and I love thee.

All the boys in our town lead a happy life,
All except Douglas - he wants a wife.
Oh, a wife he shall have, a girl of his own,
And that'll be Brenda sitting on the throne.
[faster] Oh he kissed her and he cuddled her underneath the tree,
They went down and I love thee.

3. Brown bread and brandy-o

Brown bread and brandy-o, on a summer's morning-o
If I had a watch and chain, I'd give it to my Sheila-o.
'S' stands for Sheila-o, bonnie, bonnie Sheila-o
If I had a watch and chain, I'd give it to my Sheila-o

Brown bread and brandy-o, on a summer's morning-o
If I had a watch and chain, I'd give it to my Brenda-o
'B' stands for Brenda-o, bonnie, bonnie Brenda-o
If I had a watch and chain, I'd give it to my Brenda-o.

4. Will ye lay the cushion doon?

Weet straa's dirty,
Dirties aa yer shirtie
Hie, bonnie laddie will ye lay the cushion doon?
Will ye lay the cushion doon?
Will ye lay the cushion doon?
Hie, bonnie laddie will ye lay the cushion doon?

[second voice sings "Will ye lay the cushion doon?"
Sound of laughter] Hie, bonnie laddie will ye lay the cushion doon?

Weet straa's dirty,
Dirties aa yer shirtie
Hie, bonnie laddie will ye lay the cushion doon?
Will ye lay the cushion doon?
Will ye lay the cushion doon?
Hie, bonnie laddie will ye lay the cushion doon?

5. The Hokey-Pokey

You put your right hand in,
You put your right hand out
You put your right hand in
And you shake it all about
You do the hokey-pokey
And you turn about
And that's what it's all about   Woooo!

Oh, hokey-pokey-pokey!
Oh, hokey-pokey-pokey!
Oh, hokey-pokey-pokey!
And that's what it's all about.   Woooo!

You put your left hand in,
You put your left hand out
You put your left hand in
And you shake it all about
You do the hokey-pokey
And you turn about
And that's what it's all about   Woooo!

Oh, hokey-pokey-pokey!
Oh, hokey-pokey-pokey!
Oh, hokey-pokey-pokey!
And that's what it's all about.   Woooo!

6. Meh Lad's a Terrie

Meh Meh lad's a Terrie, meh lad's a toff
Meh lad can dance like that,
Meh lad can dance like this,   [that]
He sez he loves me, I know he does
Meh lad's a Terrie toff.

Meh lad's a Terrie, meh lad's a toff
Meh lad can wear a hat
Me lad can dance like that
He sez he loves me, I know he does,
Meh lad's a Terrie toff.

7. The Banks o Aberfeldy

My father wore a rippit coat,
A rippit coat, a rippit coat,
My father wore a rippit coat,
Guess who tore it?

Ye needna hide alow the bed,
Alow the bed, alow the bed,
Ye needna hide alow the bed,
Ye dirty little toe-rag

Father, mother, may we go,
May we go, may we go?
Father, mother, may we go,
To the Banks o Aberfeldy?

Yes, indeed you may go,
You may go, you may go,
Yes, indeed you may go,
To the Banks o Aberfeldy.

Hop and skip and on you go,
On you go, on you go,
Hop and skip and on you go,
To the Banks o Aberfeldy.

Hop and skip and back you come,
Back you come, back you come,
Hop and skip and back you come,
Fae the Banks o Aberfeldy.

You dinna ken what we saw,
What we saw, what we saw,
You dinna ken what we saw,
On the Banks o Aberfeldy.

We saw a lad that danced in his kilt
Danced in his kilt, danced in his kilt
We saw a lad that danced in his kilt
On the Banks o Aberfeldy.

You dinna ken what we got,
What we got, what we got,
You dinna ken what we got,
On the Banks o Aberfeldy.

We got a kiss and a golden ring,
A golden ring, a golden ring,
We got a kiss and a golden ring,
On the Banks o Aberfeldy.

8. There Came Three Dukes a-riding

Boys:
>There came three dukes a-riding, a-riding, a-riding
>There came three dukes a-riding, ee-aye-oh

Girls:
>What d'you want with us, sir, us sir, us sir?
>What d'you want with us, sir, ee-aye-oh.

Boys, The Dukes:
>I want to marry a princess, princess, princess
>I want to marry a princess, ee-aye-oh.

Girls:
>Marry the one you're after, after, after,
>Marry the one you're after, ee-aye-oh.

Boys:
>You're all as stiff as pokers, pokers, pokers,
>You're all as stiff as pokers, ee-aye-oh.

Girls:
>Then you fell asleep, sir, asleep sir, asleep sir,
>Then you fell asleep, sir, ee-aye-oh.

Boys:
>You're all too dirty, too dirty, too dirty,
>You're all too dirty, ee-aye-oh.

Girls:
>I've got clean knees, sir, knees sir, knees, sir,
>I've got clean knees, sir, ee-aye-oh.

Boys:
> Hop around the farmers, the farmers, the farmers,
> Hop around the farmers, ee-aye-oh.

Girls:
> Hop around the farmers, the farmers, the farmers,
> Hop around the farmers, whistle and run!

SKIPPING RHYMES & SONGS

SKIPPING RHYMES & SONGS

9. A Sailor went to sea

A sailor went to sea
To see what he could see
And all that he could see
Was the sea, sea, sea!

Repeated [Oh, A sailor went to sea...]

10. Through the fields

One-two-three!
Through the fields I roam each day,
You will find me sitting on a brae,
Does she love me? Yes,
For the petals on the daisy tell me so!

[The recording has the sound double ropes as well as percussive feet.]

11. As I climbed up a Chinese steeple

When I climbed up a Chinese steeple,
There I met some Chinese people.
This is what they said to me:
"Tuppence worth o lingo, lingo, lingo,
Tuppence worth o lingo, lingo, fizz."

[Chant, to the sound of double skipping ropes]

12. Bell-bottom trousers

One, two, three! [double ropes]

Bell-bottom trousers, coat of navy blue
She loved a sailor and he loved her too.
When they get married, oh what things they'll do,
For it's bell-bottom trousers, coat of navy blue.

[repeat]

13. Brush your boots and follow

Brush your boots and follow, follow, follow,
Brush your boots and follow, don't go in.
Brush your boots and follow, follow, follow,
Brush your boots and follow, don't go in.
Brush your boots and follow, follow, follow,
Brush your boots and follow, don't go in.

[WM: "And so on...." The girls stand in a line, each waiting to jump in at the start of the rhyme and out again at the end.]

14. Down in German-ay

Down in German-ay-ay
This is what they say-ay-ay
Eeeny meeny masha,
Don't smoke Pasha
Down in German-ay.

15. Down in the meadow where the green grass grows

Down in the meadow where the green grass grows
That's where Ruth hangs out her clothes.
She sang and she sang and she sang so sweet,
Till she met her boyfriend coming down the street.
Sweetheart, sweetheart, will you marry me?
Call for the wedding at half past three.
Mummy makes Daddy call for the tea,
All for the wedding at half past three   [pause, action]Daddy
makes the dumpling, Mummy makes the tea
All for the wedding at half past three   [pause, action]
Iced cakes, iced cakes all for tea,
All for the wedding at half past three.

16. German boys they act so funny

German boys, they act so funny.
This is the way they earn their money:
Whoopalala, whoopalala,
Whoopa, whoopa, whoopalala!

17. Hill Street girls are happy

One-two-three!
Hill Street girls are happy, happy as can be,
And when they meet the Paulies they gie them one, two, three.
When the Paulies ask for mair, we say that canna be,
For we are the Hill Street girls, the Hill Street girls are we!

18. Hoppy-Hoppy is my name

One-two-three!

Hoppy-Hoppy is my name, Hoppy, Hoppy.
Hoppy-Hoppy is my name, H-O-P-P-Y

[repeated]

19. I Love Bananas

One-two-three!

I love bananas, coconuts and grapes.
That's why they call me Tarzan of the Apes.

[jump in & repeat]

20. I'm a Girl Guide

I'm a Girl Guide dressed in blue,
See all the actions I can do.
Stand at ease, bend my knees,
Salute to the King and bow to the Queen.
And turn my back on the bad sailor boy.
One, two three, a-leary
Four, five, six a-leary
Seven, eight, nine a-leary,
Ten a-leary post[man].

21. I'm a little Dutch girl

I'm a little Dutch girl, I can do the kicks
I can do the twirl-arounds and I can do the splits;
The King does this, the Queen does this
But I'm a little Dutch girl and I do this.

22. Whaur hae you been aa the day?

Whaur hae you been aa the day, bonny lassie, Hielan lassie?
Ah'll tell them: doon the brae kissin aa the laddies.

23. Jelly on the plate

Jelly on the plate,
Jelly on the plate,
Oh, wiggle waggle, wiggle waggle,
Jelly on the plate.

24. Little tin soldier stand at attention

[lines 1 & 2 sung; then chanted]

Little tin soldier, stand at attention,
Little tin soldier, stand at ease,
Little tin soldier, salute to your officer,
Little tin soldier, bend your knees. [change of pace]
Little Miss Muffet sat on a tuffet,
Eating her curds and whey.
There came a big spider and sat down beside her
And frightened Miss Muffet away.

25. Maypole butter, maypole tea

Maypole butter, Maypole tea,
M-A-Y-P-O-L-E!

[repeated 3 times]

26. She can't go to school without

One-two-three!

She can't go to school without
[boy chosen, named] Kenneth, Kenneth,
She can't go to school without
Kenneth Gray.

[repeated]

27. The Quartermaster's Store

There were rats, rats, brought in by the cats
In the store, in the store,
In the store, in the store.
There were rats, rats, brought in by the cats
In the Quartermaster's store.
My eyes are dim I cannot see,
I have not brought my specs with me,
I have not brought my specs with me.

STOTTIN THE BA:
BALL BOUNCING
GAMES

STOTTIN THE BA: BALL BOUNCING GAMES

28. Stot, stot, ba, ba

Stot, stot, ba, ba,
Twenty lassies on the Laa
No a lad among them aa,
Stot, stot, ba, ba.

29. Tensy, ninesy

Tensy, ninesy, stot the ball for eightsy,
Sevensy, sixy, stot the ball for fivesy,
Foursy, stot the ball for threesy,
Twinsy, stot the ball for onesy.

30. I'm the Monster of Blackness

I'm the monster of Blackness,
My age you'll never guess.
I can twirl in a ring, I can do the Highland Fling.
I'm the monster of Blackness.

I'm the monster of Blackness,
I bought a wedding dress,
I put it in a coffin and it fell through the bottom.
I'm the monster of Blackness.

31. Over the garden wall

Over the garden wall, I let my baby fall.
My mother came out, gave me a clout,
Over the garden wall.

32. Archibald-bald, bald

Archibald, bald, bald, King of the Jews, Jews, Jews
Bought his wife, wife, wife, a pair of shoes, shoes, shoes.
When the shoes, shoes, shoes, began to wear, wear, wear,
Archibald, bald, bald, began to swear, swear, swear.
And when the swear, swear, swear, began to stop, stop, stop
Archibald, bald, bald began to shop, shop, shop.
When the shop, shop, shop, began to sell, sell, sell
Archibald, bald, bald bought a bell, bell bell.
When the bell, bell, bell began to ring, ring, ring
Archibald, bald, bald began to sing, sing, sing.
Doh ray me fa soh lah te doh.
Who stole my wife, I do not know.

33. The London ball

    Up against the wall for the London ball,
    The London ball, the London ball,
    Up against the wall for the London ball,
    Please do pass it.   [?Pleased to pass it.]

[pause for action, then the game continues, with Part B, at a slower tempo]

    My hair is long my dress is short,
    My shoes are made of silver.
    A red, red rose upon your nose,
    And a ring upon my finger.

[pause for action, then the game continues as before]

    Up against the wall for the London ball,
    The London ball, the London ball,
    Up against the wall for the London ball,
    Please do pass it.

    My hair is long my dress is short,
    My shoes are made of silver.
    A red, red rose upon your nose,
    And a ring upon my finger.

34. Are you going to golf, sir?

Are you going to golf, sir?
No, sir. Why, sir?
Because I've got a cold, sir.
Where d'you get the cold, sir?
At the North Pole, sir.
What were you doing there, sir?
Catching a polar bear, sir.
How many did you catch, sir?
One, sir, two, sir, three, sir, four, sir,
Five, sir, six, sir, seven, sir, eight, sir, nine, sir, ten, sir,
An ever so many more, sir.

35. Charlie Chaplin went to France

Charlie Chaplin went to France,
Showed the ladies how to dance.
This is the way he taught them:
Toe, heel, tramp-aleerie,

Toe, heel, tramp-aleerie,
Toe, heel, tramp-aleerie,
That's the way he taught them!

36. Mademoiselle from Armetières

Mademoiselle from Armentières, parlez-vous.
She hadn't been kissed for forty years, same to you.
The Prince of Wales was put in jail
For riding a horse without a tail,
Inky pinky parlez-vous.

37. Alla Balla and the forty thieves

Alla Balla an the forty thieves
Stuck his nose in candle grease.
Candle grease made them sneeze,
Ali Baba an the forty thieves.

38. Robin Hood and his Merry Men

Robin Hood and his Merry Men
Went to school at half past ten.
Teacher said, "You're late again,"
Robin Hood and his Merry Men.

HAND-CLAPPING

HAND-CLAPPING

39. The bumbee stung me

The bumbee stung me, canna tell a lee,
Oh the bumbee stung me, canna tell a lee,
Oh the bumbee stung me, canna tell a lee,
For meh wee lassie's ane-twa-three.

Repeated faster, then a 3rd repeat faster still.

40. Up and down the ladder in the caravan

Up and down the ladder in the caravan,
You'll only play a penny to see the funny man.
The funny man broke and oh, what a joke!
Ha ha ha!

41. RAF o'er Berlin

RAF o'er Berlin, dropping bombs and flares
Hitler's in his shelter, shouting, 'Honey pears!'

RAF o'er Berlin, dropping bombs all day
Hitler's in his shelter, shouting, 'Are you there?'

42. Mary Queen of Scots got her head chopped off

Mary Queen of Scots got her head chopped
Head chopped off, head chopped off.
Mary Queen of Scots got her head chopped
Head chopped off!

43. Knaves and shepherds come away

Knaves and shepherds come away, come away
Knaves and shepherds come away, come away

[repeated 3 times, to the tune of 'Nymphs and Shepherds']

PLAYGROUND SONGS AND SINGING FOR FUN

PLAYGROUND SONGS AND SINGING FOR FUN

44. I'm a sailor home from sea

I'm a sailor home from sea
To see if you will marry me
Will you marry-arry-arry-arry
If you will marry me.

So you're a sailor home from sea,
To see if you will marry me,
I won't marry marry-arry-arry-arry
I won't marry you.

I give to you a silver spoon
To feed your baby in the afternoon
Will you marry-arry-arry-arry
If you will marry me.

If you give me a silver spoon
To feed my babe in the afternoon
I won't marry marry-arry-arry-arry
I won't marry you.

I'll give to you a golden gown,
To make you pretty when you go down town,
If you will marry-arry-arry-arry
If you will marry me.

If you give me a golden gown,
To make me pretty when I go down town,
I won't marry marry-arry-arry-arry
I won't marry you.

I give to you the keys to my chest,
And all the money that I possess.
Will you marry-arry-arry-arry
Will you marry me?

If you give me the keys of your chest,
And all the money that you possess
I will marry-arry-arry-arry
I will marry you.

Spoken: Ladies and gentlemen, ain't she funny,
          She doesn't want me but she wants my money

Sung: I won't marry-arry-arry-arry]
          I won't marry you!

45. Three wee wifes

Three wee wifes an three wee wifes,
An three wee wifes mak nine;
Said ae wee wife to t'ither wee wife,
"Will ye lend me yer washin line?"

Says ae wee wife tae the ither wee wife
"When will I get it back?"
Says ae wee wife tae t'other wee wife,
"Oh, Ah cannae tell ye that."

Ah hunted east, Ah hunted west,
Ah hunted Alla-balla
The only girl that I could find
Was bonnie Susie-Anna.

I took her to the ball one night
Set her down to supper,
The table fell, an she fell too
An stuck her nose in the butter.

The butter, the butter
The holy margarine,
Twa black een an a jeely nose,
An a face aa pentit green.

Her faither deh'd twa weeks ago
Left her aa his riches.
A feather bed, a corky leg,
An twa o his broken crutches.

WM: Where did you hear these songs?
DH: At the Rechabites
WM: What do they do there?
DH: We have a meeting, and then you go up onto the stage and sing.

46. I married a wife

I married a wife, oh then, oh then,
I married a wife, oh then.
I married a wife, an she couldna clean a knife
Oh the world is coming to an end.

I sent her for butter, oh then, oh then,
I sent her for butter, oh then;
I sent her for butter, an she fell in the gutter
Oh the world is coming to an end.

I sent her for cheese, oh then, oh then,
I sent her for cheese, oh then,
I sent her for cheese, an she fell on her knees
Oh the world is coming to an end.

I sent her for ham, oh then, oh then,
I sent her for ham, oh then,
I sent her for ham, an she brought back spam
Oh the world is coming to an end.

I sent her for bread, oh then, oh then,
I sent her for bread, oh then,
I sent her for bread, an she fell doon dead
Oh the world is coming to an end.

I made her a coffin, oh then, oh then,
I made her a coffin, oh then,
I made her a coffin, an she fell through the bottom
Oh the world is coming to an end.

I dug her a hole, oh then, oh then,
I dug her a hole, oh then,
I dug her a hole, an she picked up coal
Oh the world is coming to an end.

I covered her wi dirt, oh then, oh then,
I covered her wi dirt, oh then,
I covered her wi dirt, an she jumped oot her shirt
Oh the world is coming to an end.

I married another, oh then, oh then,
I married another, oh then,
I married another, she was worse than the other
Oh the world is coming to an end.

47. Poor Lady Lido

[There was a] lady dressed in green
Poor Lady Lido
There was a lady dressed in green,
Down by the greenwood side-oh.

She hud a baby in her arms
Poor Lady Lido
She hud a baby in her arms
Down by the greenwood side-oh.

She hud a breadknife sharp and lang,
Poor Lady Lido
She hud a breadknife sharp and lang,
Down by the greenwood side-oh.

She stuck it in the baby's heart
Poor Lady Lido
She stuck it in the baby's heart
Down by the greenwood side-oh.

Two loud knocks came at the door
Poor Lady Lido
Two loud knocks came at the door
Down by the greenwood side-oh.

Two big p'licemen standing there,
Poor Lady Lido
Two big p'licemen standing there,
Down by the greenwood side-oh.

He asked her what she'd done with the child,
Poor Lady Lido
He asked her what she'd done with the child,
Down by the greenwood side-oh.

Said she'd killed her only child
Poor Lady Lido
Said she'd killed her only child
Down by the greenwood side-oh.

He took her to the jail and hung her on a nail
Poor Lady Lido
He took her to the jail and hung her on a nail
Down by the greenwood side-oh.

So that is the end of the lady in green
Poor Lady Lido
That is the end of the lady in green
Down by the greenwood side-oh.

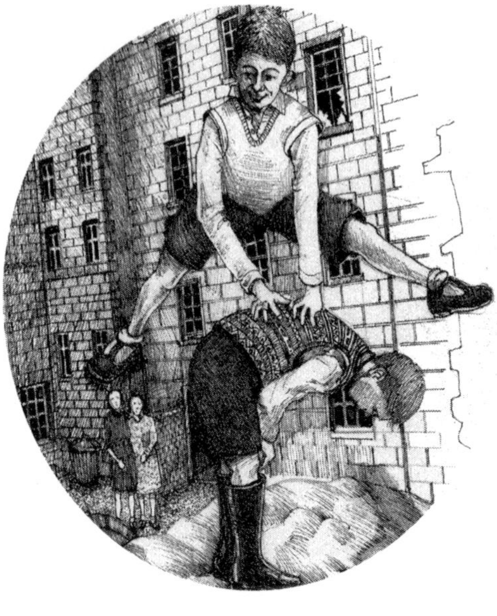

NOTES ON THE SONGS, RHYMES AND GAMES

While the notes give several cross-references to other collections and collectors, they are not intended to be an exhaustive catalogue of comparisons. Childlore research is rather like genealogical research, as no sooner do you finish the family tree than distant cousins turn up from Australia, from your grandfather's side, fifth cousins-twice removed. As Norah and Bill Montgomerie said, these songs and rhymes are 'like ambassadors' as they travel the world. The notes that follow stay closer to home, and are intended to add information about the songs, rhymes and games, the way of life of the Hilltown children, and also about the man with the tape-recorder, Bill Montgomerie, and his wife Norah.

1. Queen Mary, Queen Mary, my age is sixteen

SA1952/44/09

<http://tobarandualchais.co.uk/en/fullrecord/72313>

'Queen Mary' was already an 'old song' in the late 1800s when Alice Bertha Gomme of the Folk Lore Society invited fellow-members and friends to send her traditional children's games, rhymes and songs. She received several versions (from Northumberland to Aberdeenshire) as well as a tune. (Alice Bertha Gomme, *The Traditional Games of England, Scotland and Ireland*, Vol. 2, 1898, pp. 102–104). See also, Robert Ford's description of a girls' game which began with girls standing in a row, in *Rhymes, Children's Games, Children's Songs, Children's Stories : A Book for Bairns and Big Folk*. Paisley, 1904, p. 84.

In this singing game, the children join hands in a circle, while one girl stands in the centre. Circling around her, everyone sings, and when the tempo changes they stop for a few seconds while the girl in the centre chooses another girl. She runs in and they join hands, then they wheel round at top speed as everyone sings 'Na, na, tattie man ...' Afterwards, the first girl takes a place in the circle, and the song begins again.

See Norah & William Montgomerie, *Scottish Nursery Rhymes*, (1946), No. 156, p. 123, and *Hogarth Book of Scottish Nursery Rhymes* (1964), No 102, p. 84; James Ritchie, *The Golden City*, 1965, p. 152; Iona & Peter Opie, *The Singing Game*, 1985, pp. 239–242.

As a song, it endures beyond school age, usually without the speedy refrain. *The Greig-Duncan Folk Song Collection* has several versions and a tune, (Vol. 7, No. 1373, and Vol. 8, No. 1605) and Norman Buchan included it in 'The wee red book', *101 Scottish Songs*, (Glasgow, Collins, 1962 & 2016). His version is from a popular book of children's songs (Kerr's *Guild of Play*, published in Paisley in 1912), so not surprisingly there are only two verses – the 'naughty' verse 3 comes from the Hilltown children.

2. All the boys in our town

SA1952/44/03
<http://tobarandualchais.co.uk/en/fullrecord/72302>

Courtship games and songs have always been popular with the girls, especially when the boys are willing to join in. In this circle game, one boy, named, stands in the centre as everyone sings, circling round him. When the girls choose a partner on his behalf, they usually giggle in anticipation of the kiss, then the couple join hands and wheel round, before exiting for the next eligible bachelor. Robert Chambers refers to it as a 'Courtship Dance' and quotes a variant (*Popular Rhymes of Scotland*, 1826, p 137), and Gomme also affirms the nineteenth century popularity of kissing games (op. cit. Vol. 1, 1894, pp. 2–6).

3. Brown bread and brandy-o

SA1952/44/04
<http://tobarandualchais.co.uk/en/fullrecord/72304>

Just as one courtship game leads to another, so this one, which involves giving the gift of a watch and chain to the chosen partner. In her discussion on 'choosing partner' games, Gomme includes 18 variants, none of which includes brown bread or brandy, but have commonly grown crops for the opening line, such as, 'oats, beans, and barley grows...' (Gomme, op. cit. Vol. 2, pp. 1–13). Though a wind-up pocket watch and chain may not have much appeal in the 21st century, children in the 1950s recognised it as a symbol of status, respectability and wealth.

4. Will ye lay the cushion doon?

SA1952/44/06
<http://tobarandualchais.co.uk/en/fullrecord/72307>

This 'kissing game' was noted by Jean L. Strang in her book *Lang Strang : being a mixter-maxter of old rhymes, games etc.*, (Forfar, 1948). Her opening couplet is 'Wheat straa's dirty / Dirties aa yer shiftie', while the Hilltown children sing 'weet straa' and 'shirtie', which also rhymes.

In November 2020, when *Hilltoon lassie* Lesley McLuckie listened to the 1952 recording of 'Will ye lay the cushion doon?', she recognised it immediately: "That was a kissy game! It was sung at birthday parties – we loved playing that one! You had the cushion, and everybody sat roun in a circle, singing 'Hey, bonnie lassie, will ye lay the cushion doon?' One girl would have the cushion and she'd skip round inside the circle when everyone was singing:

> Yer shirt's aa dirty,
> Dirty aa yer shirtie
> Hey bonnie lassie will ye lay the cushion doon?

And you'd repeat that line, 'Hey bonnie lassie will ye lay the cushion doon?' till she'd laid the cushion doon at a boy that she fancied and had a kiss. And then he had to get up an lay a cushion doon at somebody else. We loved these kissing games, even when we were very young — we must have been very precocious! I can remember playin another game, 'Kissy-catchy' on the Hilltoon — at the age of five! After school, but before tea-time, on the dark winter evenings, and you were allowed out, even in Primary 1, naebody worried, cos aa the bairns were out playin. And there'd be somebody in your class that you liked and you'd be chasin them for a kissy-catchy! But we'd have tae get back fer wur tea — that was a great incentive for gettin back hame !

MB: Did you ever play 'Lay the cushion doon' in the playground?

Lesley: No, it was for birthday parties. I'm nine or ten years younger than them — I never experienced it in a playground, it was always in a house in my day. And even when you were getting a bit older, when you were a teenager, it was very exciting because somebody had picked you. [Lesley laughs] Our song began with 'Hey bonnie lassie will ye lay the cushion doon?' but I don't recognise the first line 'Weet straa's dirty .' We had, 'Yer shirt's aa dirty,' so the song went:

> Yer shirt's aa dirty,
> Dirty aa yer shirtie
> Hey bonnie lassie will ye lay the cushion doon?
> Will ye lay the cushion doon?
> Will ye lay the cushion doon?
> Hey bonnie lassie will ye lay the cushion doon?

And the next time it would be 'Hey, bonnie laddie, will ye lay the cushion doon?'

5. The Hokey-Pokey

SA1952/44/05
<http://tobarandualchais.co.uk/en/fullrecord/72305>

This is another song that may be best remembered as a party song, especially as it was also sung by grown-ups and on dance floors all over the country. The popularity among adults probably goes back to the Second World War, when Jimmy Kennedy recorded his up-beat boogie-woogie song 'Hokey Cokey' in 1941, and it rocketed into the hit parade; it was the perfect antidote to wartime worries, to cheer up the NAAFI or Saturday night dance, and everybody could join in.

By 1952 it had become so well-known that Bill Montgomerie only recorded two verses, adding "and so on ...". As anyone who has used reel-to-reel tape knows, 'saving tape' was always an issue, for it soon ran out and was expensive to buy. Nevertheless, the carefree joy of the Hilltown children can still be heard, and we can imagine them singing through the parts of the body until the last verse, 'You put your whole self in, you put your whole self out....' Their chorus is 'Hokey-Pokey' which raises an interesting point: in 1948 an American group, The Sun Valley Trio recorded it, and released it as a 78 rpm record in 1950, when it was an instant hit. The paper sleeve of the record had the words as well as actions, complete with amusing diagrams — now worth buying for the sleeve alone! <https://www.youtube.com/watch?v=RVVryacttOw>.

In 1952 Ray Anthony's 'Big Band' recorded their dance-floor hit for Capital Records with leading vocalist Jo Ann Greer and backing vocals by the Skyliners, but when their 7-inch 45 rpm record was released, the Hokey-Pokey was already a favourite in the Hilltown. And in Dundee, as elsewhere, folk were happily oblivious to the rumpus over copyright that rattled on for years.

As a singing game, the Hokey-Pokey (or -Cokey) is reminiscent of other favourites, such as 'Here we go looby-loo' enjoyed by generations of children. Many learned left from right as they acted out the song that had been around in their forebears' time – Alice B. Gomme published 20 versions and sample tunes (op. cit. Vol. 1, 1894, pp. 352–61) and Robert Chambers described a similar singing game "Hinkumbooby" played in the streets of Edinburgh and sung to the tune 'Lillibulero. (op. cit., 1826, pp. 137–139).

6. Meh Lad's a Terrie

SA1952/44/08
<http://tobarandualchais.co.uk/en/fullrecord/72311>

A 'Terrie' is the local abbreviated term for a member of the Territorial Army, which has a huge presence in Dundee. Less than two miles from Hilltown is the Dundee Territorial Army Centre, comprising extensive grounds and barracks. It is a recruiting station and training centre for several regiments, including Scotland's oldest medical unit, The Medical Support Regiment. There may be no word in the conversation of Dundonians that will identify their place of origin as quickly as 'meh'– my. The same vowel sound is echoed in other words, such as pie (peh), and can be heard in this and other songs sung by the children in Hilltown.

7. The Banks o Aberfeldy

SA1952/44/07
<http://tobarandualchais.co.uk/en/fullrecord/72309>

Apart from the opening quatrain, sung as a slow chant, the rest of the song is to the tune of 'Will Ye go to Sherriffmuir?' (widely known as the tune of 'London Bridge is Falling Down'). The first eight lines seem to have nothing to do with Aberfeldy, and there may be no obvious connection between that rural Perthshire market-town to the city of Dundee. The Birks o' Aberfeldy, a wooded area famous for its beauty, is also well-known through the song of that name composed by Robert Burns. There is no such place as The Banks o Aberfeldy – the settlement is situated to the south of the River Tay and there is no river named Aberfeldy. The town is, however, home to one of the oldest kilted regiments in the British Army, The Black Watch, and for more than a century Dundee and surrounding districts of Angus and Fife have been the main recruiting areas of the regiment. The 'lad wha danced in his kilt' may represent that connection, as there have been thousands of Dundonians who enlisted in the kilted regiment, 'proud to wear the red hackle like wir faithers an granfaithers'. (The red hackle is a bright scarlet feather plume, which is worn on the soldiers' bonnets. Among the kilted regiments it is the most distinctive feature of the Black Watch uniform, adopted in 1795 and recognised all over the world.)

There are close similarities between this song and one sung by a group of girls in Durris, Aberdeenshire, and sent (without its tune) to Gavin Greig before the First World War: "The Big Big Bunch of Roses". The opening line is "My father bought me a new topcoat," and the chorus has a similar ring to the Hilltown ditty, with "Ho-ho-ho, ye needna rin/ ye needna rin, ye needna rin, / Ho-ho-ho, ye needna rin/ For the big, big bunch of roses". It also has verses echoing the theme, "Father mother may I go?" See *The Greig-Duncan Folk Song Collection*, Vol. 8, (2002), No. 1614, p. 172.

8. There Came Three Dukes a-riding

SA1952/44/11
<http://tobarandualchais.co.uk/en/fullrecord/72317>

This courtship song has been popular among children for generations, if not centuries. As Jean L Roger describes a version from Forfar (1948, p.32) summarising the formation, it is easy to picture the children in two rows facing each other, with hands linked, advancing and retreating as they sang. The boys on one side, having chosen the three Dukes, began the dialogue while advancing towards the girls then retreating. The girls then responded as they too advanced and retreated.

Gavin Greig wrote about a version of the song entitled 'Here Are Two Dukes', sent to him by a schoolteacher from Orkney for inclusion in his column in the *Buchan Observer*. (Under the title of "Folk-Songs of the North-East" it began in December 1907 and was a regular feature until June 1911.) Greig labelled the contribution, "Children's Games and Rhymes as written down by some of the bigger pupils in Sandwick, Orkney," and included the accompanying note adding that "they are interesting and instructive as showing that this minstrelsy of the playground is largely the same in Orkney as in Aberdeenshire." (*Folk-Song in Buchan and Folk-Song of the North-East by Gavin Greig*, with a Foreword by Kenneth S. Goldstein and Arthur Argo, Hatboro, Pennsylvania 1963. See Article Number CLII.) Though Volume 7 of *The Greig-Duncan Folk Song Collection* (1997) has the entire corpus of children's songs that appeared over the years, the above note is not included. Interestingly, however, even allowing for the fact that the Orkney song has 'two Dukes arriving' (rather than 'three Dukes a-riding'), it is one of very few in the collection that was sung by the Hilltown children. The 29 versions and variants of 'Three Dukes a-riding' (as well as 4 tunes) sent to Gomme testify to the 19th century popularity of the game all over the British Isles. As she did not see all versions of the games in action, her discussion dwells on textual comparison of those sent to her, their deeper or hidden meaning (social or psychological in today's terms) and concludes with a speculative analysis of the historical significance of such games. She includes the descriptive notes sent by correspondents, mostly fellow-members of The Folk Lore Society and schoolteachers, who had watched the children play — thus we can picture the maidens curtseying as they 'look coquettishly at the dukes' who prance on their (invisible) horses and whose facial expressions show their annoyance, contempt, indignation or interest as they sing. (Gomme, op. cit. Vol. 2, pp. 233–255.) In the Hilltown, the playground and the street became the theatre, and the children were the players in a traditional musical fantasy that had a part for every child.

Within a decade of Bill Montgomerie's recording, however, the script had changed, the tune had a different tempo, and the story had been adapted for a new generation. Lesley McLuckie, who knew most of the songs, had not heard 'There came three dukes a-riding', though she lived in the Hilltown and went to school there, albeit in the late 1950s.

Lesley: We didnae dae that one, but we had 'Rosie was a lovely child' which sounds just like it.

MB: In what way?

Lesley: Everybody joined in a circle holding hands, and Rosie was in the centre — she was the Princess. We'd seen the film 'Sleeping Beauty' and we loved it. [The animated film by Walt Disney was released in January 1959.] We all wanted to be the Princess! So we had this game, and you'd go round and round, singing, and one of the boys was the handsome prince. I think we got it in school, or mebbe it was the Brownies, but we loved it, and you always hoped you'd get chosen to be Rosie, so you'd play it again, and then you could be the Princess. It went like this:

> Oh, Rosie was a lovely child, a lovely child, lovely child,
> Oh, Rosie was a lovely child, long, long, ago.
>
> Her home was in a castle, a castle, castle
> Her home was in a castle, long, long, ago.
>
> The castle walls were high, were high, were high,
> The castle walls were high, long, long, ago.
>
> A wicked fairy cast a spell, cast a spell, cast a spell,
> A wicked fairy cast a spell, long, long, ago.
>
> She went to sleep a hundred years, a hundred years, a hundred years,
> She went to sleep for a hundred years, long, long, ago.
>
> A great big forest grew all around, grew all around, grew all around
> A great big forest grew all around, long, long, ago.
>
> But a handsome Prince came riding by, riding by, riding by
> A handsome Prince came riding by, long, long, ago.

> Then he chopped those trees down one by one, one by one, one by one
> He chopped those trees down one by one, long, long, ago.
>
> He woke her with a kiss, a kiss, a kiss,
> He woke her with a kiss, long, long, ago.
>
> And then they got married, got married, got married,
> And then they got married, long, long, ago.
>
> Now everybody's happy, happy, happy,
> Now everybody is happy, long, long, ago.

That might not be all of it, but it's most of it, and everybody got a wee part, even if it was just being the proverbial dramatic, tree waving your branches around in the circle. The wicked fairy was a great part too, cos she acted out the spell-casting, but of course everybody wanted to be the Princess. And when it came to the bit when the Princess got wakened with a kiss, we'd all go [making the sound of a kiss]!

Playground games have an enormous contribution to make to the performing arts: among their peers children are free to express themselves without inhibition, sing at the tops of their voices, prance, jump, twirl, pull faces, collapse in laughter, or act silly. Outside the humdrum of daily life, there's also the chance to enjoy being a Duke or a Princess and to be celebrated by everyone.

9. A Sailor went to sea

SA1952/45/01
<http://tobarandualchais.co.uk/en/fullrecord/72321>

Despite the absence of photographs or film, the recording of 'A sailor went to sea' picks up the metronomic sounds of skipping ropes and feet — a skipping song, without a doubt. The same song, sung to a different beat and in staccato style is also widely known as a hand-clapping song. As a folklorist interested in the performing arts, I have used this song with students at the Royal Conservatoire of Scotland (formerly the Royal College of Music and Drama), as we 'discover' the universality of traditional songs. "Does anyone know any clapping songs?" I ask, eliciting the same chorused response over twenty years: 'A sailor went to sea'. I then explain (as if for the first time) it was not one I had seen in the 1950s or '60s, so I invite volunteers to demonstrate. To the surprise of the class, several discoveries are made: very few boys played it (so far not one has volunteered), almost all the city girls played it, though it's not so well-known in rural areas, whether in Scotland, Ireland, England, Wales, Poland, Sweden, Canada, America, Australia or Japan.... It seems to be everywhere and (to their surprise) pairs of players from different countries could adapt to each other, while students who had never played this found it difficult to learn; and percussionists and pipers invariably drum out the beat with their fingers. The laughter and animated discussion usually opens up an opportunity to consider the importance of childlore as the early training for a myriad of skills. Have a go! <http://funclapping.com/song-list/a-sailor-went-to-sea/>

10. Through the fields

SA1952/45/24
<http://tobarandualchais.co.uk/en/fullrecord/72360>

11. As I climbed up a Chinese steeple

SA1952/45/02
<http://tobarandualchais.co.uk/en/fullrecord/72323>

Bell-bottom trousers

SA1952/45/04
<http://tobarandualchais.co.uk/en/fullrecord/72326>

'Bell Bottom Trousers' was the title of a World War 2 song written by Lithuanian-American composer Moe Jaffe. It was recorded in 1944, sung by Connie Boswell to be issued on a V-disc (for U.S. military personnel) and sent out to military bases and naval vessels to boost morale. With its theme of true love and loyalty the song was instantly popular on both sides of the Atlantic. The following year it was recorded commercially by Guy Lombardo and The Royal Canadians. The backing had the sound of a brisk, naval marching band, and their 7-inch 45rpm took off, rocketing the song to the top of the 1945 hit-parade.

Moe Jaffe later admitted the idea wasn't entirely original – he based it on a slightly bawdy broadside ballad he had heard in which a young maid, seduced by a sailor, is left to face the consequence. Although there seems to be no mention of where Jaffe heard the song, or who sang it, it had already been recorded by Herbert Halpert, who made a recording in 1941 of a singer in Bloomington, Indiana singing 'Bell-Bottom Trousers', which he described as a 'bawdy sailor song'. Halpert's fieldwork recordings which include this song were made on 12-inch 78rpm acetate discs and were later deposited in the Archives of Traditional Music at Indiana University. (6 hour-long discs; see catalogue of contents and access to audio: <https://iucat.iu.edu/catalog/13956820)>

It is fairly likely, however, that 'Bell Bottom Trousers' reached the Hilltown via the radio, as the 2-line chorus of the hit-record is the same as the opening couplet of the four-line ditty sung by the children.

Brush your boots and follow

SA1952/45/05
<http://tobarandualchais.co.uk/en/fullrecord/72323>

Down in German-ay

SA1952/45/06
<http://tobarandualchais.co.uk/en/fullrecord/72330>
'Pasha' is Turkish tobacco

Down in the meadow where the green grass grows

SA1952/45/07
<http://tobarandualchais.co.uk/en/fullrecord/72332>

'Down in the Meadow' was already 'old' when Gomme published several versions in *Traditional Games*, Vol. 1 (1894) pp. 99–100 and Vol. 2 (1898) pp. 416–18. The Opies also have several versions in *The Singing Game* (Oxford, 1985), pp. 127-130, as do several other collectors. Ewan McVicar notes: "'Down in yonder Meadow' is a fine example of the collector's dictum that even if you recognise several opening lines you should never say 'I already know that one.'" *Scots Children's Songs and Rhymes: Doh, Ray, Me, When Ah Wis Wee*, (2007), pp. 192–93. As with many songs and rhymes, 'Down in the Meadow' set off on a voyage with thousands of emigrants and turns up generations after sailing ships landed in ports around the world.
Thanks to audio-recordings made by Herbert Halpert, we can still listen to the voices of a group of girls in North Carolina in 1939 singing 'Down in the meadow where the green grass grows'. During the Great Depression Halpert recorded widely in North Carolina and other areas settled by Scottish and 'Scotch-Irish' immigrants in the 1700s. His acetate discs recorded in North Carolina can be heard via Indiana University's 'Halpert Mid-Atlantic Collection' <https://libraries.indiana.edu/halpert-midatlantic>.

The version Bill Montgomerie recorded in Dundee reflects a time when weddings were celebrated in local church or co-operative halls, and all the catering was done by the family. The appearance of lavish wedding cakes is comparatively recent, and a 'clootie dumpling' was generally made for the occasion. Much loved all over Scotland, it's a 'well-known fact' that, wherever you live, everybody's Mammy (or Daddy) makes the best clootie dumpling.

German boys they act so funny

SA1952/45/08
<http://tobarandualchais.co.uk/en/fullrecord/72333>

Hill Street girls are happy

SA1952/45/09
<http://tobarandualchais.co.uk/en/fullrecord/72333>
The 'Paulies' were the boys from a nearby St Peter & St Paul R.C. School.

19. Hoppy-Hoppy is my name

SA1952/45/10
<http://tobarandualchais.co.uk/en/fullrecord/72337>

I Love Bananas

SA1952/45/11
<http://tobarandualchais.co.uk/en/fullrecord/7233>

When the National Film Corporation of America released the silent movie 'Tarzan of the Apes' in 1918, it was a sensational box office success. Cinemas all over Scotland featured the film, so, unsurprisingly, Tarzan soon made his way into songs of school playgrounds and city streets. Enthusiasts of old movies may watch it via the internet, and those who prefer to read the book will find that Edgar R. Burrough's *Tarzan of the Apes* has never been out of print since 1912.

I'm a Girl Guide

SA1952/45/12
<http://tobarandualchais.co.uk/en/fullrecord/72340>

Girl-Guiding has been popular in Dundee for over 100 years, and the Hilltown Company is one of ten in the city. As variants of this skipping rhyme turn up all over the English-speaking world, so also do they feature in most collections of childlore. Too many to mention, they are cited by Janet E. Alton and John D.A. Widdowson in their annotation of Nigel Kelsey's mammoth collection (1966–1984), *Games, Rhymes, and Wordplay of London Children*, (Centre for English Language Heritage, Edale, 2019), pp. 291–94.

I'm a little Dutch girl

SA1952/45/13
<http://tobarandualchais.co.uk/en/fullrecord/72342>

Alton and Widdowson annotate multiple variants of 'I'm a Little Dutch Girl', op. cit., pp. 200–203.

Whaur hae you been aa the day

SA1952/45/26
<http://tobarandualchais.co.uk/en/fullrecord/72362>

To the tune of 'Hieland Laddie'

23. Jelly on a plate

SA1952/45/14
<http://tobarandualchais.co.uk/en/fullrecord/72343>

24. Little tin soldier stand at attention

SA1952/044/047
<http://tobarandualchais.co.uk/en/fullrecord/72347>

25. Maypole butter, maypole tea

SA1952/044/047
<http://tobarandualchais.co.uk/en/fullrecord/72350>

From the late 1800s, 'Maypole' was the name of a well-known a supplier of dairy produce. The 1909–1910 Post Office phone-book for Dundee list two branches of the 'Maypole Dairy Co.' at 64 High Street and 3 King's Road.

26. She can't go to school without

SA1952/45/22
<http://tobarandualchais.co.uk/en/fullrecord/72358>

The tune is part-A of 'Camptown Races' with its 'Doodah, doodah!' refrain which lends itself to teasing songs.

The Quartermaster's Store

SA1952/45/23
[Not included on Tobar an Dualchais]
A version of 'The Quartermaster's Store', sung as a brisk march, became popular during the First World War and was also a favourite with the Boy Scouts. Though the Hilltown children sang only one verse, there are many which can be spontaneously sung, or made up, to lengthen the song and add to the fun.

Stot, stot, ba, ba

SA1952/45/32
<http://tobarandualchais.co.uk/en/fullrecord/72372>

The 'Laa' is Dundee Law, a volcanic plug which is Dundee's most distinctive landmark. It gives its name to the surrounding area of the city, where the children lived and went to school. Gomme included a Fraserburgh version of the rhyme, sent to her by the Rev. Walter Gregor: 'Stot, stot, ba', ba' /Twenty lassies in a raw…' Vol. 2, 1898, p. 406.

Tensy, ninesy

SA1952/45/33
<http://tobarandualchais.co.uk/en/fullrecord/72373>

Lesley McLuckie recalled a row of girls chanting this rhyme as they stotted the ball following a sequence of movements: under one leg, then the other, clapping hands, twirling round, without missing a beat.

I'm the monster of Blackness

SA1952/45/19
<http://tobarandualchais.co.uk/en/fullrecord/72352>

Not to be outdone by Highlanders who boast a world-famous monster, Nessie, the Hilltown children sing of their own monster, located in the area of Dundee known as Blackness. The recording picks up the accuracy of their ball-bouncing as they never miss a beat as they 'stot the ba'. In the last line, a few children can be heard singing 'Loch Ness'.

Over the garden wall

SA1952/45/20
<http://tobarandualchais.co.uk/en/fullrecord/72354>

Archibald, bald, bald

SA1952/45/34
<http://tobarandualchais.co.uk/en/fullrecord/72374>

In this version, the last couplet is sung up and down the scale. See also Ritchie, *The Golden City*, p. 135.

The London ball

SA1952/44/02
<http://tobarandualchais.co.uk/en/fullrecord/72300>

Are you going to golf, sir?

SA1952/45/28
<http://tobarandualchais.co.uk/en/fullrecord/72364>

Chanted while stottin the ball; see also Ritchie, *The Golden City*, p. 85

Charlie Chaplin went to France

SA1952/45/29
<http://tobarandualchais.co.uk/en/fullrecord/72366>

Though Charlie Chaplin was a star of silent movies, his popularity lives on in the playground, even among children who have never seen the movies. The Opies collected several variants from many parts of Britain (*Lore and Language of Schoolchildren*, 1959, pp 108–10), and James Ritchie collected two variants in Edinburgh. Ritchie refers to Charlie Chaplin as 'the one and only hero' of the silent movies. *The Singing Street*, pp. 23–24.

Mademoiselle from Armentières

SA1952/45/30
<http://tobarandualchais.co.uk/en/fullrecord/72368>

'Mademoiselle from Armentières' became popular during World War 1 when it was recorded c. 1915 by music-hall singer Jack Charman (Decca Records) and other recording artists. The song, or versions of it, has been sung ever since, parodied in barracks and bars, trenches and on route marches, through World War 2, and inevitably turns up in the playground where it serves to keep time to a ball-bouncing routine.

Alla Balla an the forty thieves

SA1952/45/27
<http://tobarandualchais.co.uk/en/fullrecord/72363>

Robin Hood and his Merry Men

SA1952/45/31
<http://tobarandualchais.co.uk/en/fullrecord/72368>

Edinburgh children also sang a ditty about Robin Hood and his merry men; see Ritchie, *The Golden City*, p. 144.

The bumbee stung me

SA1952/44/10
<http://tobarandualchais.co.uk/en/fullrecord/72315>

The tune is reminiscent of 'Up Amang the Heather on the Hill o Bennachie' which also features a bumbee (bumble-bee). The song works equally well for skipping, with two girls 'cawing' the rope while the others stand single file in a queue. One girl jumps in, while all sing the song, repeating it faster and faster, till the player trips, laughter ensues, then the next person jumps in.

Up and down the ladder in the caravan

SA1952/45/25
<http://tobarandualchais.co.uk/en/fullrecord/72361>

RAF o'er Berlin

SA1952/45/21
<http://tobarandualchais.co.uk/en/fullrecord/72356>
Text and music transcribed for 'Tocher' 14, 1974. 1 verse. Children's skipping rhyme

The Opies published a version from Dundee that begins, 'RAF o'er Berlin / Dropping bombs in play...' *Lore and Language*, 1959, p.102.

Mary Queen of Scots got her head chopped off

SA1952/044/047
<http://tobarandualchais.co.uk/en/fullrecord/72348>

Knaves and shepherds

SA1952/45/15
<http://tobarandualchais.co.uk/en/fullrecord/72345>

To the tune of Henry Purcell's 'Nymphs and Shepherds', the children sing only the first two lines, which are repeated as they play. It is impossible to know if any of them were aware that their song is a parody.

44. I'm a sailor home from sea

SA1952/46/05
[Not included on Tobar an Dualchais]
Sung by Ruth Husband and Moira MacDonald, aged 9

'I'm a sailor home from sea' has a long and varied history and it turns up under many titles. Widely known in the English-speaking world as 'Paper of Pins' it is generally sung as a duet, a dialogue between a boy and a girl (or a group of each), with 'question and answer' verses. As the title has so many variants it can be misleading, but the common theme is 'if you will marry me,' or a polite invitation to courtship, 'if you will walk with me.' Norman Buchan included it in his 'wee red book', with the title 'If you Will Marry Me', noting that it is a Glasgow street song. *101 Scottish Songs*, (Glasgow, 1962), p. 143. There is no mention of a sailor, but one turns up in a version collected by Nigel Kelsey in a London playground in 1974. The title is 'I'm a sailor young and gay' and Kelsey notes that the children told him it was adapted from a song they had learned in the classroom. (Alton & Widdowson, 2019, pp. 231–33)

This begs the question, is it in a school song-book somewhere, with the sailor the main character? In Bill Montgomerie's recording the girls in

Hilltown sing it like a parlour-room duet, in over-articulated posh voices — in local terms 'they're awfie pan-loaf' so I asked the Hilltoon lassie, Lesley, to comment. "That was all part of the game! We loved to pretend we were posh and so we'd speak in a pehn-loaf way and that was all part of the fun." The duet, as a performance, is reminiscent of the polite style of a kirk soiree, similar to a song recorded in Aberdeen by Alan Lomax in 1951. Mr & Mrs John Mearns sang 'I'll gie ye a pennyworth o preens' in the style of a genteel, drawing-room duet — it has the same question-answer pattern, a different tune, and the last (and crucial) question concerned the 'key o ma heart' which is graciously accepted, and the final verse is sung as a vocal harmony affirming the happily-ever-after outcome. (Lomax donated copies of his Scottish recordings to the Archives of the School of Scottish Studies, accessioned on SA 1951/14/A115, B1. Listen online via the Lomax Archive: <http://research.culturalequity.org/rc-b2/get-audio-detailed-recording.do?recordingId=12156>)

The Hilltown version, however, was not one the girls learned in a school classroom, as they sang two verses (not included here) which were not suitable for the school concert or the kirk soiree.

The Montgomeries, however, collected and published two versions of 'I'll gie ye a pennyworth o preens', including one with 17 verses, published in their first book, *Scottish Nursery Rhymes* (Hogarth, 1946), Number 86, pp 74–77, and another with 11 verses, published in *Traditional Scottish Nursery Rhymes*, (Edinburgh 1986), Number 67, pp. 45–46. They are similar in 'plot' with minor differences in language use, with offers of a 'bonnie siller box' and, curiously, the 'hauf o Bristol town, wi coaches rollin up an doun.' While it is impossible to discover the origin of such lines, it is interesting to find the verses in Robert Chambers' *cante fable*, entitled 'The Tempted Lady'. As the story goes, 'there was ance a leddy, and she was aye fond o being brawer than other folk...' and she meets with a gentleman, 'nae gentleman in reality, but Auld Nick himsel ... [he had] cloven feet, but he keepit them out o sight.' Then the courtship begins, in song: 'I'll gie you a pennyworth o preens', with several other offers and refusals until (verse 11) she is offered the 'hauf o Bristol town, wi coaches rollin up an doon.' The leddy asks for 'the hale o Bristol toun,' and she is granted the request. The song ends with her acceptance and the narrator returns to announce that the devil (Auld Nick) flies off with her, concluding with the warning, 'Noo, lasses, see ye maun aye mind that.' (Edinburgh, 1826).

45. Three wee wifes

SA1952/46/04
<http://tobarandualchais.co.uk/en/fullrecord/72384>
Sung by David Husband, aged 11.

The 4-line verse beginning 'Her faither deh'd twa weeks ago' was also collected by the Montgomeries as a separate rhyme (or chant); see *A Book of Scottish Nursery Rhymes*, Hogarth Press, 1963. No 172, p. 126.
The temperance organisation known as 'The Rechabites' was set up to combat problems of alcoholism among workers. They had an affiliation with the church-based 'Band of Hope' and The Boys Brigade.

See Tocher, No.44, 1992, p.119, with musical transcription by Alan Bruford.

46. I married a wife

SA/1952/46/03
<http://tobarandualchais.co.uk/en/fullrecord/72380>
Sung by David Husband, aged 11.

James Ritchie recorded a very similar version in Edinburgh, which he includes in a section of 'guising ballads' sung at Hallowe'en when the children were out guising and asked to sing. *The Singing Street*, p. 115.

47. Poor Lady Lido

SA1952/44/01
[Not included on Tobar an Dualchais]
Sung by Charles Allardyce, aged 14.

'Poor Lady Lido' is a version of the ballad, 'The Cruel Mother', which, in spite of (or perhaps because of) the morbid story-line, has long been a favourite among children. Since the publication of F. J. Child's seminal work, the ballad has also been of interest to song collectors and scholars all over the world. Lancashire-born Anne G Gilchrist (1863 – 1954), who was an avid member of The Folk Song Society and contemporary of Cecil Sharp, Ralph Vaughan Williams and Percy Grainger, recalled that her father used to sing a version which began, 'There was a lady dressed in green' – he had a 'burring R in the choruses' which he insisted that the children should keep. Both parents were Scottish and had a wide variety of songs, many of which were central to her research. She cited this song as evidence that some children's songs evolved from old ballads, and from 1948 to 1952 corresponded with Bill Montgomerie. (He later donated eleven letters to the Archives of the National Library of Scotland: <https://manuscripts.nls.uk/repositories/2/resources/10370>.)

Fifteen years after Bill Montgomerie recorded 'Poor Lady Lido', a version of the same ballad suddenly swept into concerts and folk clubs across the world, and frequently featured on radio and TV after The Clancy Brothers recorded "Weelia, weelia, wyia' in 1965. The Dubliners sang their gravelly version in 1966, and to this day, thousands of 'folkies' still join in the song, which begins 'There was an old woman who lived in the woods ...' It's the same story of cruelty, so in the end 'they put a rope around her neck' and 'she gets hung,' so 'that was the end of the woman in the wood...'

The Hilltown children also sing the refrain, 'Poor Lady Lido', and after listening to them Bill Montgomerie asked the soloist about it:

Wm Montgomerie:	Well, now, where did you hear that?
Charles Allardyce:	In Bridge of Weir Orphanage
Wm Montgomerie:	And who was singing it?
Charles Allardyce:	The boys in the orphanage
Wm Montgomerie:	Thank you very much.

Their conversation seems as eerie as the song, but there is no further information about the repertoire of the children's orphanage, or about when the singer relocated to Dundee.

It was Bill Montgomerie's quest for Scottish ballads that prompted him to take a year out from his teaching job in 1952, to make fieldwork recordings and to devote time to completing his Ph.D. on ballad manuscripts. His interest dated back to the mid-1920s when he was a student and introduced to the work of Harvard ballad scholar Francis James Child (1825–96), whose monumental 5-volume collection, *The English and Scottish Popular Ballads*, is now regarded as the most important work ever produced — the 'bible' of international ballad scholarship, with "Child-numbers" (1–305) as crucial to the researcher as "The Periodic Table of Elements" is to the chemist. Professor Child had collaborated with international scholars to collect and compare ballads that shared a common story, regardless of language or location — for example, an anonymous poem learned in school, 'The Twa Corbies', turns up under the heading of 'The Three Ravens' and is number 29 in Child's collection. We may wonder why 'three', and not two corbies or ravens? The poem Bill learned at school appears in Professor Child's collection, quoted from Walter Scott's *Minstrelsy of the Scottish Borders*, alongside another poetic version of the same story featuring three ravens. A simple discovery about a poem, or ballad, led to Bill's intensive study of the Scottish manuscripts cited by Child. He came to the conclusion that Professor Child was too narrow in his views as he was an 'armchair scholar' who concentrated on manuscripts, and seemed oblivious to the fact that these old songs were still being sung in Scotland. Furthermore, Child had ignored manuscript versions that had been noted from the singing of children. It was as if they didn't exist, and so in 1952 Bill set out to record songs, hoping that, among them, there would be some that matched those numbered in the collection of Child Ballads. The first gem was 'Poor Lady Lido' sung by a laddie in the Hilltown, and while the story is fairly gruesome, the song is a version of 'The Cruel Mother' (known internationally as 'Child 20'). Traditional songs and ballads are alive and well in Scotland, and the children in the Hilltown are a testimony to oral transmission.

In the weeks that followed Bill's fieldtrip to the Dundee playground, he took his tape-recorder up the Angus glens and along the coast to Arbroath. On a dozen reel-to-reel tapes he recorded 117 items, which included nine Child ballads: 'Lord Donald' (Child 12, 'Randal'); 'Son David' (Child 13, 'Edward'); 'Poor Lady Lido' (Child 20, 'The Cruel Mother'); 'The Twa Brithers' (Child 29); 'The Battle o Harlaw' (Child 163); 'Mary Hamilton' (Child 173); 'Oh, waly, waly up yon bank..." (Child 204, 'Jamie Douglas'); 'Bonnie George Campbell' (Child 210); and 'The Dowie Dens o Yarrow' (Child 214). Most of the adult singers were farm labourers, fisherfolk and their families, and through their songs we get a sense of the communities in which they lived, the cultural and social setting, the labour history, the relevance of the songs to the people who sang them. The children in Dundee also created a vibrant soundscape of the Hilltown, with their songs, rhymes, games and laughter a lasting reminder of the importance of childlore in retaining traditions as well as to general well-being.

As Percy Grainger aptly put it over a century ago, audio-recordings capture not 'merely the tunes and words of fine folk-songs, but [also] an enduring picture of the lives, art and traditions ... of singing ... the dialects of different districts ... vocal habits and other personal characteristics of singers'.

FURTHER READING & LISTENING

Books and cassettes for children, parents and teachers

Montgomerie, William & Norah. 1946. *Scottish Nursery Rhymes*, London: The Hogarth Press.

Montgomerie, Norah & William, 1948. *Sandy Candy and other Scottish Nursery Rhymes*, London: The Hogarth Press.

Montgomerie, Norah & William, 1956. *The Well at World's End: Folk Tales of Scotland Retold*, London, The Hogarth Press.

Montgomerie, Norah & K. Lines (illustrated by N. Montgomerie), 1959. *Poems and Pictures*, London, Abelard-Schuman.

Montgomerie, Norah, 1961. *Twenty-five Fables*, London, Abelard-Schuman

Montgomerie, Norah (author and illustrator), 1964. *The Merry Little Fox, and Other Animal Stories*, London, Abelard-Schuman.

Montgomerie, Norah & William, 1964. *The Hogarth Book of Scottish Nursery Rhymes*, London: Hogarth Press.

Montgomerie, Norah & William, 1964. *The Hogarth Book of English Nursery Rhymes*, London: Hogarth Press

Montgomerie, Norah (ed) & M. Gill (illustrator), 1965. *To Read & To Tell: An Anthology of Stories for Children*, London: Bodley Head.

Montgomerie, Norah, 1967. *One, Two, Three. A Little Book of Counting Rhymes*, London: Abelard-Schuman.

Montgomerie, Norah (ed) & T. Jordan (illustrator), 1971. *More Stories to Read and to Tell*, London: Bodley Head.

Montgomerie, Norah & William, Marjery Gill, 1975. *The Well at the World's End: Folk tales of Scotland*, London: Bodley Head.

Montgomerie, Norah (author & Illustrator), 1983. *This Little Pig Went to Market: Play Rhymes for Infants and Young Children*, London: Bodley Head.

Montgomerie, Norah & William, 1985 & 1990. *Traditional Scottish Nursery Rhymes*, Edinburgh, Chambers.

Montgomerie, Norah & William, 1985 & 1992. 'Scottish Nursery Rhymes and Verses' and 'The White Pet', Whigmaleerie Audio Books for Children Edinburgh: Canongate Audio Cassettes.

Montgomerie, Norah & William, 1993. *The Well at the World's End* : Folk tales of Scotland, Edinburgh: Canongate Silkies.

Montgomerie, Norah & William, 2005. *The Folk tales of Scotland: The Well at the World's End and other stories*, Edinburgh: Mercat Press; Birlinn, 2008.

Montgomerie, Norah, illustrated by P. Rumsey, J. Brooks (ed.), 2009 *Fantastical Feats of Finn MacCoul*, Edinburgh: Birlinn.

Poetry by William Montgomerie

Montgomerie, William, 1933. *Via: Poems,* London: Boriswood.

Montgomerie, William, 1934. *Squared circle. A vision of the Cairngorms.* London: Boriswood.

Montgomerie, William, 1970. *A selection of three poems: Storm from the south, Rhyme from the German, Epitaph,* Dundee: Duncan of Jordanstone College of Art.

Montgomerie, William, 1985. *From Time to Time: Selected Poems,* Edinburgh: Canongate.

Montgomerie, William, 2005. 'Flodden' in M. Lindsay & L. Duncan (Eds.), *The Edinburgh Book of Twentieth-Century Scottish Poetry,* p. 250. Edinburgh: Edinburgh University Press.

Montgomerie, William, 2013. 'Broughty Ferry' and 'Lifeboat Disaster, April 1960' in W. Herbert & A. Jackson, (Eds.), *Whaleback City: Poems from Dundee and its Hinterlands,* pp. 11 and 100-106. Dundee: Edinburgh University Press.

(Many others; see Scottish Poetry Library catalogue, online)

Research contributions by William Montgomerie (selection)

Montgomerie, William (ed.), 1947. *New Judgments: Robert Burns: Essays by six contemporary writers*, Glasgow: William Maclellan.

Montgomerie, William, 1955. 'The Twa Corbies.' *The Review of English Studies*, 6(23), 227-232.

Montgomerie, William, 1953. 'Bibliography of the Scottish Ballad Manuscripts, 1730-1825' unpublished PhD dissertation, The University of Edinburgh.

Montgomerie, William, 1956. 'Folk Play and Ritual in *Hamlet*.' *Folklore*, 67 (4), 214-227.

Montgomerie, William, 1956. 'Sketch for a History of the Scottish Ballad.' *Journal of the English Folk Dance and Song Society*, 8 (1), 40-43.

Montgomerie, William, 1956. 'Sir Walter Scott as Ballad Editor.' *The Review of English Studies*, 7 (26), 158-163.

Montgomerie, William, 1958. 'William Motherwell and Robert A. Smith.' *The Review of English Studies*, 9 (34), 152-159.

Montgomerie, William, 1963. 'William Macmath and the Scott Ballad Manuscripts.' *Studies in Scottish Literature*: Vol. 1: Iss. 2, 93–98.

Montgomerie, William, 1967. 'A Bibliography of the Scottish Ballad Manuscripts 1730-1825: Part I, *Studies in Scottish Literature*: Vol. 4: Iss. 1, 3–28.

Montgomerie, William, 1967. 'A Bibliography of the Scottish Ballad Manuscripts 1730-1825: Part II.' *Studies in Scottish Literature*: Vol. 4: Iss. 2, 79–88.

Montgomerie, William, 1967. 'A Bibliography of the Scottish Ballad Manuscripts 1730-1825: Part III.' *Studies in Scottish Literature*: Vol.4: Iss. 3, 194–227.

Montgomerie, William, 1967. 'A Bibliography of the Scottish Ballad Manuscripts 1730-1825: Part IV,' *Studies in Scottish Literature*: Vol. 5: Iss. 2, 107–132.

Montgomerie, William, 1968. 'A Bibliography of the Scottish Ballad Manuscripts 1730-1825: Part V.' *Studies in Scottish Literature*: Vol. 6: Iss. 2, 91–104.

Montgomerie, William, 1969. 'A Bibliography of the Scottish Ballad Manuscripts 1730-1825: Part VI.' *Studies in Scottish Literature*: Vol. 7 Iss. 1, 60–75.

Montgomerie, William, 1970. 'A Bibliography of the Scottish Ballad Manuscripts 1730-1825: Part VII.' *Studies in Scottish Literature*: Vol. 7: Iss. 4, 238–254

Citations and sources

Baron, R., 2010. '"I Saw Mrs Saray, Sitting on a Bombalerry": Ralph Ellison Collects Children's Folklore.' *Children's Folklore Review*, Vol. 32, pp. 23–52.

Bennett, Margaret, 1992. '[A Tribute to] William and Norah Montgomerie.' *Tocher*, 44, pp. 117–124.

Bennett, Margaret, 2019. 'Corbies and Laverocks and the Four and Twenty Blackbirds: The Montgomerie Legacy to Folklore and the Mother Tongue.' *Tradition Today*, Issue 9, June 2020, pp. 1–22. Online journal: http://centre-for-english-traditional-heritage.org/TraditionToday9/1_Bennett.pdf

Bishop, Julia C., 1998. 'Dr Carpenter from the Harvard College in America: An Introduction to James Madison Carpenter and His Collection.' *Folk Music Journal*, vol. 7, no. 4, pp. 402–420.

Broadwood, Lucy E., Percy Grainger, Cecil J. Sharp, Ralph Vaughan Williams, Frank Kidson, J. A. Fuller-Maitland, and A. G. Gilchrist, 1908. 'Songs Collected by Percy Grainger.' *Journal of the Folk-Song Society*, vol. 3, no. 12.

Bronson, Bernard H, 1959. *The Traditional Tunes of the Child Ballads*, Princeton, N.J.: Princeton University Press.

Buchan, Norman, 1963. *101 Scottish Songs*, Glasgow: Collins. Many re-prints; re-launched by the Traditional Music and Song Association (TMSA) in 2016.

Campbell, John Lorne, and Hugh Cheape, 2000. *A Very Civil People: Hebridean Folk, History and Tradition*. Edinburgh: Birlinn.

Chambers, Robert, 1826. *Popular Rhymes of Scotland*, Edinburgh: W. & R. Chambers. London and Edinburgh, 1840, 1858, 1870.

Child, Francis James, 1882–1898. *The English and Scottish Popular Ballads*. Five volumes, Boston and New York: Houghton, Mifflin and Co., Reprint edition, hardbound, New York: Cooper Square Publishers, 1962, Reprint edition, New York: Dover Publications, 1965.

Collinson, Francis M., 1958. Reviewed Works: 'The Twa Corbies', 'Sir Walter Scott as Ballad Editor', 'William Motherwell and Robert A. Smith' and 'Some Notes on the Herd Manuscripts' by William Montgomerie.' *Journal of the English Folk Dance and Song Society*, 8, no. 3, p. 170.

Freeman, Graham, 2009. '"That Chief Undercurrent of My Mind": Percy Grainger and the Aesthetics of English Folk Song.' *Folk Music Journal*, vol. 9, no. 4, pp. 581–617.

Goldstein, Kenneth S. & Arthur Argo (eds), 1963. *Folk-Song in Buchan and Folk-Song of the North-East by Gavin Greig*, Hatboro, Pennsylvania: U. Penn. Press.

Gomme, Alice Bertha, 1894 and 1898. *The Traditional Games of England, Scotland and Ireland*, 2 vols., London: The Folklore Society.

Grainger, Percy, 1908. 'Collecting with the Phonograph.' *Journal of the Folk-Song Society*, Vol. 3, No. 12, pp. 147-162.

Grider, Sylvia Ann, 1980. 'A Select Bibliography of Childlore.' *Western Folklore*, 39, no. 3, pp. 248–265.

Halpert, Herbert, 1982. 'Childlore Bibliography: A Supplement.' *Western Folklore*, 41, no. 3, pp. 205–28.

Kay, Billy, 1986. *Scots: The Mither Tongue*, Edinburgh: Mainstream.

Kelsey, Nigel (collector), Janet E. Alton & John D.A. Widdowson (editors), 2019. *Games, Rhymes, and Wordplay of London Children*, (Centre for English Language Heritage, Edale).

Kennedy Fraser, Marjorie with Kenneth MacLeod (translator). 1909–1921. *Songs of the Hebrides and Other Celtic Songs from The Highlands of Scotland*, 3 Vols., London: Boosey & Hawkes.

Lomax, Alan, 1955. 'World Library of Folk & Primitive Music: Scotland', Volume 3, Columbia Records.

Lomax, Alan, 2004. 'Singing in the Streets: Scottish Children's Songs' from the Alan Lomax Collection; selection and notes by Ewan McVicar, Rounder Records, Cambridge, Mass.

Lovelace, Martin, Paul Smith, and John D.A. Widdowson (editors), 2002. *Folklore: An Emerging Discipline, Selected Essays of Herbert Halpert*, St. John's, Canada: MUN Folklore and Language Publication.

Lyle, E.B., Crawfurd, A. & Scottish Text Society, 1975. *Andrew Crawfurd's Collection of Ballads and Songs*, Edinburgh: Scottish Text Society.

McCarthy, William B., 1990. *The Ballad Matrix: Personality, Milieu, and the Oral Tradition*, Bloomington: Indiana University Press.

McVicar, Ewan, 2007. *Scots Children's Songs and Rhymes: Doh, Ray, Me, When Ah Wis Wee*, Edinburgh, Birlinn.

Olson, Ian A., 1998. 'Scottish Song in the James Madison Carpenter Collection.' *Folk Music Journal*, vol. 7, no. 4, pp. 421–433.

Opie, Iona & Peter, 1959. *The Lore and Language of Schoolchildren*. Oxford: OUP.

Opie, Iona & Peter, 1985. *The Singing Game*. Oxford: O.U.P.

Porter, James & Herschel Gower, *Jeannie Robertson: Emergent Singer, Transformative Voice,* Knoxville: University of Tennessee Press, 1995.

Purves, David, 1997. *A Scots Grammar: Scots Grammar and Usage.* Edinburgh: The Saltire Society, Revised Edition, 2002.

Ritchie, James T. R., 1964. *The Singing Street.* Edinburgh and London: Oliver and Boyd.

Ritchie, James T. R., 1965. *The Golden City.* Edinburgh and London: Oliver and Boyd.

Roud, Steve, 2010. *The Lore of the Playground: One hundred years of children's games, rhymes and traditions,* London: Random House Books.

Shuldham-Shaw, Patrick., Lyle, Emily B., et al., 1981–2002. *The Greig-Duncan Folk Song Collection,* 8 Vols., Aberdeen: Aberdeen University Press & The Mercat Press.

Strang, Jean L., 1948. *Lang Strang: being a mixter-maxter of old rhymes, games etc.,* Forfar: Forfar Press.

Taylor, Archer, 1949. 'Review of Scottish Nursery Rhymes.' *The Journal of American Folklore,* 62, No. 244, pp. 214–214.

Wolz, Lyn A., 2005, 'Resources in the Vaughan Williams Memorial Library: The Anne Geddes Gilchrist Manuscript Collection.' *Folk Music Journal,* 8, no. 5, pp. 619–639.

Yates, Michael, 1982. 'Percy Grainger and the Impact of the Phonograph.' *Folk Music Journal,* Vol. 4, No. 3, pp. 265–275.

Online resources

Alan Lomax Archive: <http://research.culturalequity.org/rc-b2/get-audio-detailed-recording.do?recordingId=12156>

Anne Geddes Gilchrist Papers in the Vaughan Williams Memorial: <https://www.vwml.org/record/AGG>

Archives of Traditional Music at Indiana University: https://libraries.indiana.edu/halpert-midatlantic and 'Halpert Mid-Atlantic Collection': <https://iucat.iu.edu/catalog/13956820>

Education Scotland: <https://education.gov.scot/education-scotland/news-and-events/keeping-the-mither-tongue-alive-celebrating-minority-languages-in-all-their-diversity-and-distinctiveness/>

National Library of Scotland: The William Montgomerie papers: Included are 11 letters written by musical antiquary Anne Geddes Gilchrist (1863-1954) to William Montgomerie between 1948-1952, concerning literary and musical matters, (Presented to the NLS by William Montgomerie, Edinburgh, 13 June 1978.) <https://manuscripts.nls.uk/repositories/2/resources/10370>

The University of Edinburgh, Archives of the School of Scottish Studies: Tobar an Dualchais/Kist o Riches. <http://www.tobarandualchais.co.uk/>

The Scottish Poetry Library, Dian Montgomerie Elvin: Biography of William Montgomerie. <https://www.scottishpoetrylibrary.org.uk/poet/william-montgomerie/>

FIRST LINE OF SONGS

A sailor went to sea	49
All the boys in our town lead a happy life	40
Alla Balla an the forty thieves	66
Archibald, bald, bald, King of the Jews, Jews, Jews	62
Are you going to golf, sir?	64
Bell-bottom trousers, coat of navy blue	50
Brown bread and brandy-o, on a summer's morning-o	40
Brush your boots and follow, follow, follow	51
Charlie Chaplin went to France	65
Down in German-ay-ay	51
Down in the meadow where the green grass grows	52
German boys, they act so funny	52
Hill Street girls are happy, happy as can be	52
Hoppy-Hoppy is my name, Hoppy, Hoppy	53
I love bananas, coconuts and grapes	53
I married a wife, oh then, oh then	78
I'm a Girl Guide dressed in blue	53
I'm a little Dutch girl, I can do the kicks	54

I'm a sailor home from sea	75
I'm the monster of Blackness	61
Jelly on the plate	54
Knaves and shepherds come away, come away	71
Little tin soldier, stand at attention	55
Mademoiselle from Armentières, parlez-vous	66
Mary Queen of Scots got her head chopped	71
Maypole butter, Maypole tea	56
Meh lad's a Terrie, meh lad's a toff	43
My father wore a rippit coat,	43
Over the garden wall, I let my baby fall	62
Queen Mary, Queen Mary, my age is sixteen	39
RAF o'er Berlin, dropping bombs and flares	70
Robin Hood and his Merry Men	66
She can't go to school without	56
Stot, stot, ba, ba	61
Tensy, ninesy, stot the ball for eightsy	61
The bumbee stung me, canna tell a lee	69
There came three dukes a-riding, a-riding, a-riding	45
There was a lady dressed in green	80

There were rats, rats, brought in by the cats	57
Three wee wifes an three wee wifes	77
Through the fields I roam each day	49
Up against the wall for the London ball	63
Up and down the ladder in the caravan	70
Weet straa's dirty	41
Whaur hae you been aa the day, bonny lassie, Hielan lassie?	54
When I climbed up a Chinese steeple	50
You put your right hand in	42

CONTRIBUTORS

WILLIAM MONTGOMERIE (1904–1994) was born and brought up in Glasgow. After graduating from the University of Glasgow, he became a teacher and moved to Dundee, where he met and married NORAH Shargool (1909–1998), an artist with D.C. Thomson. They shared a passion for the Scots language and folklore and published many books for children. William Montgomerie was also a renowned poet and ballad scholar, and, though he was a pioneer in tape-recording traditional songs and folklore, this is the first time any of his recordings have been published.

MARGARET BENNETT is a folklorist, writer, singer and storyteller. Born in 1946, she grew up in Skye, trained as a teacher, then studied Folklore. Widely regarded as "Scotland's foremost folklorist", she lectured at the The University of Edinburgh School of Scottish Studies (1984–96) before joining the part-time staff of the Royal Conservatoire of Scotland (Glasgow). A prize-winning author and singer, she is dedicated to handing on Scotland's traditions to new generations. Margaret is also Honorary Professor of Antiquities and Folklore at the Royal Scottish Academy (Edinburgh) and Honorary Teaching Fellow at the University of St. Andrews. She is interested in sharing community folklore and oral history projects for all ages and abilities, and in contributing to media research. As Hamish Henderson wrote, "Margaret embodies the spirit of Scotland." <www.margaretbennett.co.uk>

Born in 1947, LES MCCONNELL hails from Ayrshire. He studied at Edinburgh College of Art and was awarded a graduate scholarship to study in Holland. Les trained as a teacher and settled in Fife, where, in retirement his pencils and artist's palette are part of daily life. He has exhibited widely, including at the RSA, and his recent collaborations with Fife poet William Hershaw, include *The Sair Road*, depicting striking images from Fife's mining industry, and *Saul Vaigers*, following the pilgrimages of Scottish saints. Their joint exhibition 'Earth Bound Companions' (2019) was reviewed with critical acclaim and will be published as a poetry pamphlet by Grace Note Publications.

ACKNOWLEDGEMENTS

In preparing this collection for publication I have enjoyed many hours of listening to the voices of the children in Hilltown, Dundee. For several decades I have felt that 'somebody ought to publish them', and consider myself fortunate to have known the 'man behind the microphone', William Montgomerie, as well as his wife Norah. Over thirty years ago they gave me a cassette copy of the original 1952 tape-recordings, and though I had hoped to work with them to produce an audio-recording for distribution, success eluded us. Nevertheless, the dream did not fade, and neither did my enthusiasm, which was revived earlier this year when Professor Emeritus John D. W. Widdowson of The National Centre for English Cultural Tradition invited me to contribute an article about the Montgomeries' contribution to childlore. I appreciate John's interest, as my fellow-folklorist in Sheffield reminded me of the importance of William and Norah Montgomerie's work to folklorists and linguists all over the English-speaking world.

I am grateful, therefore, to the Royal Conservatoire of Scotland and to Grace Note Publications for supporting the production of this collection, which will hopefully bring pleasure to many as well as provide a resource for teachers, performing artists, social historians, folklorists, linguists and Scots language enthusiasts.

My debt of gratitude to the Montgomeries goes back many years and fortunately I was able to express it to William (Bill) and Norah. I would like to thank their daughter, Dian Montgomerie Elvin for her permission to publish the recordings and for her encouragement and friendship over those years. I am grateful to Dr Cathlin Macaulay and to Stuart Robinson at the Archives of the School of Scottish Studies in Edinburgh for providing a digital version of the tape-recordings and also for guiding me through 'the paperwork'. While working on the project I had hoped to find someone who grew up in Hilltown, and was fortunate to be introduced to Lesley McLuckie, a retired school-teacher, a 'real Hilltoon lassie' and a singer, who shared her childhood memories. Thank you, Lesley!

At each stage of writing I have been assisted by Russell and Ros Salton, who have read and re-read many drafts, proof-reading each page with patience and good humour that lit up many hours at my desk. If any errors have crept back in, they are entirely my own, and I would like to accord my profound thanks to Ros and Russell for all their support and friendship.

Gonzalo Mazzei of Grace Note Publications introduced me to artist Les McConnell and I was delighted he agreed to collaborate. I am extremely grateful to Les, who entered into the spirit of the playground and added enormous pleasure to the entire project with his emotive illustrations. Finally, I would like to accord my heartfelt thanks to Gonzalo, who typeset and designed the book, and finalised the production of the CD.

As Charlie Chaplin wrote, "A day without laughter is a day wasted", to which I might add, a day without gratitude is also a day wasted.

Margaret Bennett, 2021.